THE GIRL WHO SWALLOWED THE MOON

THE GIRL WHO SWALLOWED THE MOON

MELANIE GIDEON

ASTARTE SHELL PRESS

PORTLAND MAINE

Astarte Shell Press, Inc.
P.O. Box 10453
Portland, Maine 04104

Library of Congress Cataloging-in-Publishing Data
Gideon, Melanie, 1963-
The girl who swallowed the moon/Melanie Gideon
p. cm.
ISBN 0-9624626-9-1: $12.95
1. Saint George River (Maine)—Fiction.
2. Young women—Maine—Fiction. I. Title.
PS3557. I255G57 1994
813'.54—dc20 94-35002
CIP

Cover illustration and book design by Sylvia Sims, Portland, Maine
Typesetting by Eleanor Haney, Bath, Maine
Printed in the USA by McNaughton & Gunn, Saline, Michigan
on recycled paper

First printing 1994

10 9 8 7 6 5 4 3 2 1

ACKNOWLEDGEMENTS

I wish to thank all the women at Astarte Shell Press, especially Sapphire and Sylvia Sims, for their talent and insight, their belief in me and in this book; Sally Brady, my agent, for her continual support; everyone who helped get this book out into the world in some way: Ellen Ames, Laura Barnard, Alexandra Merrill, Jan Schmidt, Jessie Shefrin, the folks at Thinking Machines, and Benjamin Hunter Rewis, who brought me to the river.

DEDICATION

This book is dedicated with great love to my grandmothers, Azbar and Sunite, and my mother, Sarah.

TABLE OF CONTENTS

PART ONE

AT THE RIVER

One night she began to remember. This was the night she tipped her head up to the darkness and howled.

Mistaking her for a wolf, a sliver of the moon came down from the thick night sky, where it poured into her open mouth like liquid—silver, then yellow, then gold. The moon was cool and tasted clean, like stone, and when it reached her womb it transformed itself from a glimmering stream to a fingernail of moon. It bounced a few times as it settled in. Nestled into the firm pink walls. And sighed.

The girl heard that sigh. And it was then that she began to listen. The sound of the moon sighing in her body was like nothing she had ever heard. It was the softest and deepest sound imaginable. It was a rumbling, a stirring, an ache. Her body was pulled. Every molecule pulled toward that center where the moon now lived. Like a great wind, it sucked her to her middle and it was there that she found the silence.

And then the remembering.

1

It was morning when Arian finally left the hill. She waited until the sun rose, and when she felt it warm on her face, she began the walk home.

It was the beginning of August and the smells of summer were heavy. Pollen, flowers and roots, the smells so thick it was almost possible to see them, like an invisible smoke. The smell was the result of bright sun and short, but powerful rains. The earth was brilliantly green. Abundantly full.

Arian reached down and felt her stomach. It was flat. She lifted up her shirt and exposed her skin to the air. It was warm, but no warmer than usual. After a few minutes she noticed a beat, a pulse, coming through. She smiled. She knew last night had not been a dream. She could tell by the way she was walking. She was gliding across the land.

She was not sure what would happen now, but she did know one thing. She was to wait. She headed back to the house, humming, singing some bit of a song and making up the words. Feeling the life rocking in her belly. Feeling the gold bounce up and down and sway as she picked up her skirt and ran.

The moon bounced when Arian ran and began to laugh. The laughter was contagious and the girl felt it rise from her belly to her throat where it came out her mouth in a beautiful, long string of jewels. Rubies, emeralds and sapphires. They spilled out and glistened in the sun. They fell from the girl's mouth into the arms of the earth and came to rest finally in the rich brown soil.

Arian was beautiful. She had always been beautiful, but now her beauty was deepening. If you happened to see her running down the hill that morning, her skirt blown up and her legs long and reaching, you would say, yes, yes, that girl is beautiful. And as she got closer you would see the sparks of red, blue and green falling from her lips as she laughed. Then you would hear the laughter.

And you would wonder if you had ever really heard laughter before because her laugh was so much. Her laugh was the sound of the sky at dusk, blue and purple, so clean and clear, bittersweet in its slow turning to black. These were the jewels that spilled from her lips. This was the sound of her laughter.

The land began to level out and Arian followed the sounds of the water back to the river. She walked close to the edges where the ground was soft, almost muddy. Soon, the house was in sight. She felt enormously happy at the sight of the gray, weathered shingles. The river house was waiting for her.

The house was perched on large, flat rocks on the banks of the St. George river in Maine. You could dive into the water from the front porch which overlooked the most tender and delicately curved part of the river. This part was the river's foot. Elegantly extended, the arch was high and beautiful, and this part of the river wrapped right around the cabin. It was not by accident that the house happened to be there.

The river was particularly long and particularly beautiful on that early spring day, in 1892, when Lena Finn finally got the courage, the help and the strength, to drag her creaking old body and her beloved house down the bank and into the water where, miraculously, it floated like a bird.

Nobody could believe it. They all stood there with their mouths open as Lena stood on the front porch staring back at them. She had known it would float. It was the house's destiny as well as her own to move downstream. And when the village finally came together that day—humoring the old woman, because maybe if they tried, she would put the idea to rest—the house slid right off the land and into the river with only the mildest of pushes, as if it had been waiting and ready for a long, long time.

It landed with a soft plop in the water, with barely a splash, and just bobbed up and down as if saying in its own quiet way, "I told you so." Lena spoke to the house then as if she was speaking to a child about to go on a journey. She spoke quietly and under her breath, and nobody heard what she said. People told stories that she was speaking some magic, some incantation. But really what she said was short and to the point.

She said, "House, it's time." And that was all that was needed. The house turned around slowly and started moving downstream.

The ice had finally broken, and the first purple crocuses were sticking their tight heads out from the muddy earth on that spring day, and Lena had listened closely to the river's song. There were many beautiful places she was tempted to put her house to rest, but she listened to the river and the river kept telling her to wait. She was old and tired, and sailing to what she knew was to be the last place she would live on this earth, and she was glad when she finally reached the foot of the river and the wind changed direction, neatly depositing both herself and the house on shore.

Arian loved Lena's house from the first minute she saw it. It probably started before then, as soon as she set foot on the dirt road that led through the woods to the river. For as soon as she had taken her first step up that road, Arian began to change. She began to become the girl she once was.

Arian knew in her heart that this was the last time she would truly be a girl, for in less than one month she was to be married. This time at the river was her Aunt Naomi's wedding present to her. Arian had protested at first, but eventually gave in, because when she had finally stopped saying no, she heard the river singing in her head. So she had packed her bags and gone. At the end of the dirt road she had found the house.

"I'm here," Arian said, putting her bags down on the porch, inhaling the clean, warm smell of river water. She shook her head as she spoke those two words out into the silence, knowing they were tiny words, but powerful somehow, powerful enough to set planets into motion. If she had thought more about it, she might have stopped herself from speaking aloud, but the words flew out of her mouth as fast as fate. And once they were in the air, it was too late. Because two small words were all it took for that house to wake up.

House stood perfectly still. *Something* was happening. *Something* that felt like an itch.

House was remembering. Remembering what it was to speak, trying to remember how to pull her voice up through her foundation and send it whistling through her wooden walls. She used to be very good at it. But that had been many years ago. One hundred to be exact, and House had pretty much given up on a second coming. So when Arian first began to talk to her, she found herself unable to respond.

Arian tried again.

"I've come," she said, this time her voice shaking. House began to sweat, she tried to pull herself out of the old rocking chair. She hadn't stood in so long. She'd better get up fast, though. House could tell by the sound of Arian's voice that if she didn't answer now, the girl would give up and go away.

House knew that Arian was calling from a place deep inside her; she was in the process of remembering how to speak a language her soul had forgotten.

It was a place that most people never knew existed. This girl was not only aware of its existence, but had figured out how to re-enter that place and then stand in it. She was standing there, a little wobbly perhaps, but standing nonetheless, when her voice came out and summoned House from her hundred-year sleep.

House had no choice then, but to remember how to speak, so strong was the pull in Arian's voice—the voice that asked her to come back into the world, that demanded her participation.

Arian and House were both slow the first couple of days with the language, neither having spoken it in many years. House soon found, though, that she was able to carry on as smoothly as she had with Lena.

Arian had a harder time. It seemed to House that the girl's problem was that she *thought* too much about speaking the language, instead of just doing it.

It wasn't about thinking at all, and House knew Arian would

soon figure that out. The language was not something to be learned. It never had been and never would be. There would be no point to it if it had to be taught.

No, it was something in the bones. Something buried deep in the genes, in the cells. Everyone was born knowing it, it was just a question of when it was lost. All babies could talk to the trees, that was common knowledge. But usually, near the age of three, the language was forgotten—*persuaded* out of them, actually, and in its place there was taught a more "appropriate" way of conversing.

The trees never got used to it. They would go on calling to the children long after the children stopped answering. The trees didn't seem to mind, though, because once in a blue moon a child would remember, and that seemed to make it all worth while.

House heard Arian's yell in the distance. She looked up. Finally, the girl had returned. She had been out all night. House had been worried. It was only Arian's third day here, after all, and House felt responsible for her safety.

House watched her closely as she ran up the hill, and immediately she knew that something had happened. Something very big.

To begin with, Arian was speaking the language, and there was no effort, no straining. There weren't the visible signs on her face — the furrowed brow, the closed eyes, the concentration and the reaching to break through.

There was, in its place, the whisper of her words. Like a song it was, effortless once it was remembered. Tripped by that one line, those two or three notes, it all came flooding back. It was the remembering that was so painful and awkward, like learning to walk.

Arian came running up the hill, her cheeks darkening, flushed apricot.

"Welcome home, Arian," said House, when she stepped on the porch.

Arian smiled and nodded, tipping back on her heels, her head moving into the light.

House pushed open the screen door and let her in.

It was more than House could have dreamed. She had known there was something special about Arian the first moment she saw her, but to think this girl had hidden in her the power to swallow the moon—it was almost inconceivable. Still, she knew it was true. Arian was marked. She had silver and gold dust around the corners of her mouth.

Moondust was something rarely seen. House had only seen it once before. True, she was no expert, but she prided herself on the clarity of that memory. It was a sight she would never forget.

Lena had not been able to fall asleep that night, so she and House prepared to sit and watch the morning come in. It was a cold, clear winter evening. Bright, even though there was no moon—the sky a pale orange.

It happened around three in the morning. Lena and House had been sitting quietly for awhile, listening to the sounds of the fire. Already that night there had been much laughter, much whooping and hollering, letting loose. Lena said the darkness always made her do crazy things.

"What kind of things?" asked House innocently, baiting her.

"Well, things I wouldn't normally do in the light, of course," answered Lena.

Then the noise came. It was a loud bump, a settling in, and it sounded as if it was right up on the porch outside.

Lena sat forward in her chair, her eyes wide and curious.

"Lena, don't even think about going outside," House said in a firm voice. Lena didn't seem to hear her. This always happened. In times of danger Lena would stop listening to House and just do whatever she wanted. She was stubborn. This did not please House. Lena was not as young as she used to be, certainly not of an age to be tangling with whomever or whatever was out on that porch.

"Lena, don't go!" House yelled, but it was too late. Lena was already standing up, the afghans falling to the floor.

Lena walked to the front door slowly and surely. House had to give her credit, she was a stately old bird. Lena began to open the door and House couldn't help it, she yelled one last "No!" The door opened halfway into the winter night, hit something hard and solid, and then stopped. Cold air came funnelling into the room.

This seemed to bring Lena out of her trance and she turned back to House with a small smile and said, "I think we're going to be all right, House."

Whatever gave her that idea, thought House, more than a little bit annoyed. House didn't like the way the door wasn't moving. Something was blocking the door. Something was lying on the porch and that something was alive. House was quite nervous and visibly shaking now. Bits of snow from the roof were falling, giving the illusion of a flurry.

"Oh, don't be such a baby, House," said Lena.

At that remark, not about to be outdone by Lena's display of courage, House came up right behind her and the two of them peeked around the corner into the night.

At first there wasn't much to see. It was dark on the porch. Then House heard the breathing, quiet and deep. House's first instinct was to turn and run, but Lena held her back.

"No, wait," she said. "I don't think it means to hurt us."

Lena pulled House up beside her. Together they pushed the door open, sliding whatever lay in front of it slowly around, so the door could fully swing on its hinges.

"Slowly, now," coached Lena. "We don't want to scare her. . . slowly."

The black lump of an animal lay in front of them, her snout at their feet. It took a few minutes for their eyes to become accustomed to the dark and then they realized they were looking at a wolf.

House, Lena and the wolf sized each other up. Lena noticed that the wolf was aware of House's presence behind her, which made her feel completely safe. She could see the wolf's eyes taking inventory, going back and forth between Lena and House, trying to figure out if she had made a good choice about collapsing on their porch.

Lena was good at reading animals. This wolf was obviously one who understood the language, and even though she didn't appear to be hurt, there was something strange about her. Something not quite ordinary. Then they noticed her mouth. It was glowing.

It was a bright night. Perhaps that's why it showed up as well as it did that evening. Or maybe it was just because they had never seen the glow of moondust before. The way it glimmers from underneath. The way it sticks to the corners of the mouth. Regardless, those shiny, translucent, golden-silver flecks of precious moon stopped Lena and House dead in their tracks.

"House," whispered Lena.

"What?" came back the stunned reply.

"Do you see what I see?"

"Around her mouth?"

"Yes."

Lena wanted so much to take her finger and wipe the edges of the wolf's mouth, where the stuff seemed to be dripping so that she might feel the texture of moondust, so she might rub it in the palm of her hand. But she knew the moondust was not hers to take. She would have to content herself with just the sight of it.

House and Lena stayed with the wolf on the porch until it was morning. They watched over her as she slept, never taking their eyes off that brilliant mouth, the gleaming and dancing moondust lodged in the pink and black spotted gums that would mark her forever as chosen.

"Might as well wear a sign on your neck," said Lena to House in a whisper. "Saying the Moon was here. Ah, yes, she was here."

The wolf woke up then, eyed them both, and with a friendly flick of her tail trotted off slowly into the growing day. Lena and House looked carefully to see if any flecks of moondust might fall off behind her, but if any did, they just melted right into the snow.

So, for the second time in her life, House stood staring moondust in the face, and it was perhaps even more shocking than the first.

What had the girl gotten herself into? Speaking the language was one thing, but swallowing the moon, that was an entirely different story. As far as House knew there had never been a human who had swallowed the moon. Certainly there had been some who had tried, but they ended up kind of crazy, preaching gibberish and all sorts of nasty stuff.

House looked over at Arian. The girl looked exhausted.

"Come on," said House, "time to rest."

Arian looked at her gratefully and smiled, silver and gold dancing off her lips. House swept Arian up into her arms, aware that she was carrying a most precious cargo, girl and moon, and gently laid her down on the bed. Arian was asleep in minutes. House did not leave her side.

2

It had been a beautiful night, that night just past, the sky deep and black, so deep that Arian pushed her arm through it and felt it thick and moist, wrapping like a mitten around her hand.

Arian had always felt most comfortable outside, in the woods. She could feel things there she didn't feel anywhere else. Nothing was taken for granted. The pine needles were a bed. The breeze was her mother's hand on her forehead.

But never had she run her fingers through the dark and felt the stars slipping over her fingernails like ice. This was different. She trusted it, and it told her to move, to travel. She knew that wherever she was going she had never been there before. But she knew that she must go.

With that thought, she felt the fear start, felt it come on in and circle round her, and she stopped. She would lose the way if she gave in to the fear. Of this she was certain. Her fear would not lead her to where she must go—her faith would.

And so, after a time, she talked herself out of the fear and began walking again. Sure enough, her feet knew the way. They remembered. *She* remembered.

She remembered what it was like to be the dark. And she wrapped herself around herself, blanketed herself in the sweet molasses batter. She borrowed night's cloak and threw it over her shoulders. She looked magnificent, striding through the woods, traces of pink and purple sky streaming out behind her.

Wearing night's cloak gave her the courage to keep walking. Because she wasn't walking *in* the night. She *was* night. And she was no longer afraid. She looked down at her feet, saw them walking quickly, surely, firmly. She looked down at her feet and she loved those feet. She looked down at her hands, each one of them wrapped with rich sticky darkness and icy blue stars. She looked down at those hands and she loved those hands. And she looked down at the curve of her belly, at the small, earth-colored breasts, at the tips of her hair hanging over her shoulders and she loved her belly, her breasts and her hair.

And it was the night. It was night that handed those things to her, gave them back to her like a gift. She saw herself then, for the first time, in the dark, and she loved herself without a doubt.

She carried herself, carried the night on her back. She carried them both through the forest and into a clearing where the noises were loud all around her.

The crickets sang of moist, green places, their songs right on the edge, where sad melts into sweet. It was a song of remembering, she realized. The crickets sang the taste of corn, yellow and bursting with buttery silk. They sang the smell of strawberries in warm rain. They sang the song of mist, of morning, of twilight. They sang to help her remember.

Arian kneeled down in the clearing and listened and finally heard the crickets' song. She let it pull her. She fell backwards into it. It was comforting and it was safe.

And she remembered.

The sky was dark purple, black around the edges. It shivered and danced. Loving herself ferociously, she took the sky in her two hands and pulled it down to her like a sheet. She folded the sky in half. It was big, this sky, cool and cavernous, like a shell. She stepped into it, one foot at a time, like she was stepping into pajamas. She pulled the sky on, brought it up around her waist and knotted it like a sash.

She was dressed. It suited her. She wore only the sky, slung low around her hips and the night as a cape on her back. Her legs were strong and firm. Her shoulders wide, a contradiction to her long, beautifully-arched neck. Her lips curved down at the edges and were the color of raspberries. She was slim, muscled, and she ran like an animal, low to the ground and leaping, one hand sweeping her long hair into a tail as she flew. She smelled like pine sap, she smelled like rock. She wore the sky and the night with the ease and familiarity of a second skin and she was all of these things and more.

Standing now, she lifted her head up. She was intensely aware of every part of her body, every stretch, every tendon. She could feel her bones settling within her skin, felt the skin holding her tight. It felt wonderful, the pull of her neck. Slowly and deliberately, she moved her eyes upward.

And saw the ladder, hanging like a planet in the sky.

3

It was time for that girl to eat some food, House thought.

She was watching Arian. The girl was finally awake, but still she lay there on the bed, her body stiff and unmoving. She was deep in some other place.

House decided the girl needed a break. One could only take so much swallowing of moons and wearing of the sky. It was time for some food, for some gossip and laughter, perhaps a game of rummy.

She hovered over Arian's head to feel the temperature of her breath. It was hot, and she didn't even notice House right there in her face.

"Arian, how about something to eat?" whispered House in her ear.

Arian didn't say anything. House looked into her eyes.

"Arian, come on, get up now, you need something to eat." This time House's voice was firm. Arian turned her head to face House.

"Everything hurts," she said. "My neck, my legs, my back. I don't think I can move."

She looked exhausted, thought House, but not beyond recovery.

House recognized her symptoms. Lena used to get the same way. Arian was in need of remembering that she was human and that meant doing something real and solid. Eating, bathing. Walking and moving about.

House lifted her up tenderly in her arms. Arian nestled her face into House's shoulder.

"That's right, that's right," murmured House, "You're going to be just fine."

House walked outside with her into the late afternoon sunshine. Arian blinked and covered her eyes.

"It hurts, House," she whined. Her voice was hoarse and scratchy. "The sun hurts."

House walked with Arian down to the dock and held her, rocking her like a child. She began to sing. She sang every song that she knew, and when she had run through her entire repertoire, she went through it again. It was vital that she bring Arian back into balance. To help her remember where she was from.

Arian needed to remember that she had a complete life waiting for her on the other side of the road. It would be dangerous if Arian sank so deeply into House's world that she forgot where she had come from. Arian was only here for a short moment in time, and no matter how much she might like to stay, she was not meant to. She had come to this world *only* to move into her future.

Finally, Arian began to unfold. Her fists loosened and her breath became even and sweet. She took her hand away from her eyes and let the late day sun blanket her face. After a time she looked much better, almost peaceful. There was even a small smile on her face. House had brought her back.

River, who had been watching, waiting until the hard moments had gone by, came creeping up to the sides of the dock then, silently and a bit timidly. She waited awhile, until she felt it was the right time, and then stuck her head up over the edge.

"Let me take her," she whispered. "Please."

She held her hands out for the girl. River's voice was like liquid, her hands wide and moving.

"Yes," said House. "Help me get her undressed."

With a gentle touch, House and River undressed Arian. "That feels wonderful," said Arian, delighting in the air on her body as each piece of clothing came off. Being undressed made her feel like a child.

And when she was naked, House leaned down and placed her in River's arms. River was right there to catch her. Slowly, she dipped her in. First her toes, then her hands. An ankle, a knee and a back. Finally, when she was used to the temperature, River lowered her down into her depths.

Feeling as though she were melting, Arian was blissful; she had never been so lovingly held, bathed and carried; never had she felt so beloved.

She started to cry, soft, silent tears at first, that mixed with River. She cried with her eyes wide open, the water running into the corners of her raspberry lips. She cried, not moving, her body still in River's arms.

River tasted her tears and pressed them to her chest. She took Arian's face in her hands and held it, catching the tears before they fell. And when Arian felt her touch, when she felt the warm hands of River on her face, something inside her released, and she began to sob, her shoulders shaking and heaving.

Watching from the bank, House's first instinct was to grab Arian up and protect her. She sat quiet for a moment though, and thought better of it, realizing the girl needed badly to cry—to cry for not knowing what was to happen, to cry for feeling so deeply and so exquisitely it was as if she were on fire. These tears were precious and they were needed. So House only watched.

River was an expert at tears. They were, after all, what she was made of. She was a giant collection of tears. Tears as old as the sky, frog tears, fish tears, beaver tears. But mostly what River was made of—what made her so wide, so warm and so moving—were mothers' tears. And mothers' tears, perhaps, meant the most of all. Because they were made up of everything there was. They were complete and they were full, because they were tears of a lifetime.

They were tears of making love. Tears at the intensity of the womb shaking and quivering, of the miracle of one body inside another. Of feeling two hearts slam up against one another and beat and flutter and cry out with the pain and unfairness of being separated by flesh.

They were the tears of giving life. Of the swollen feet, the back that wants to collapse, the nipples that darken and spread. Of the breathing, of the pushing, of the ripping and the tearing. Of the stretch of legs pulled so wide they feel like they will split.

Tears of how are we going to pay for this winter jacket, of baby skin that smells of powder and strained apricots. Of a child's head heavy in a lap. Tears of swimming under the dock, of tender, new breasts, of sneaking in the house after midnight. Tears of *I hate you.* Tears of *I love you.* Tears of pulling back and letting go.

Of pulling back. Of letting go.

And River bathes her. River bathes her in her past and in her future. In her waters, past and future are not separate. They are not different. In the river they are one.

She has a strong back, this River. So she takes yet one more set of tears. She holds them tight to her chest, as she has all the others, and then she lets them go.

She does not make Arian feel guilty for crying. She does not try to wipe away the snot that comes with the heaving. She just holds Arian's face in her hands and lets this girl cry.

4

It was a plain ordinary ladder, made of wood. It floated ten feet off the ground in front of her, the color of bleached bone.

This was her ladder. She knew it as she had never known anything else. She wore the sky on her hips and the night on her back, she loved herself without a doubt. It was hers.

She closed her eyes and took a giant step into the dark, up into nothingness, her hand outstretched. At first she felt nothing beneath her feet. Nothing but air. She started to panic, but forced herself to keep reaching. You can do this, she whispered to herself. You know how. *Remember.* Finally, eventually, she felt wood. She grabbed the wood and pulled herself up, waited until both feet were firmly planted on a rung, then opened her eyes.

At first, she was so scared she just looked straight ahead through two rungs, her hands gripping the wood so tightly they lost their color. After a few minutes, she began to relax and noticed a few things. The wood of the ladder was polished smooth and white. It smelled clean and stiff, like shirts on a clothesline. She even tested her weight and pushed forward a bit to see if the ladder would sway. It did not. It was firmly planted in the middle of the sky.

She mustered up her courage, reminded herself she was not afraid of heights and looked up. What she saw amazed her.

When she had been on the ground, looking up at the ladder, it had looked small, maybe eight feet tall. Now that she was on it, she realized that it was enormous. It stretched for what looked like miles into the night in front of her. Suddenly she felt despair drop like a shovelful of dirt onto her faith. Voices began rising in her chest. *You can't do this,* they said. *You will fall.* They began to plan, to plot, to move right in and stop this silly nonsense. The girl felt weak, dizzy. She stopped believing for a second and that was all it took. The ladder began to sway, it began to turn in the sky. And it began to disappear.

She screamed when she felt the wood under her fingers become air and she began to slide down the ladder. She didn't want to go, but she didn't know how to stay—how to stop the voices, how to stop the fear.

Then the wind stepped in. It flew down like a big white bird, and sat on the girl's shoulder and whispered to her of faith. It spoke to her of belief. It took those other voices and blew them clear across the world to China. The girl laughed then, and finally, together, they took that shovelful of despair and sent it flying.

There was silence. The ladder was firm under her hands. In the silence the night began to stir on her back. The sky wrapped around her legs.

She began to climb.

5

Arian had shown House the book the night before she swallowed the moon.

"I wanted you to see this," she said, and opened the book of fairy tales. "When I was young I would spend hours looking at this picture."

House took the book into her lap. It was a drawing of a princess and a stag with ruby-studded antlers. The princess was sad, her eyes were big and gray. She was slender and wore a crown on her head. Her gown was spun gold and her waist-length hair was the color of new dimes.

"They are brother and sister," explained Arian. "He was put under a spell by his stepmother. I used to think, back then, that if I stared hard enough into this picture, I would eventually fall right in."

"You see, I wanted to live in a world where girls had quests." Arian looked out the window for a moment and then sat back down in her chair and sighed. "Those worlds exist you know, House. You just have to find the way in."

Arian pulled her chair up close to House.

"There are entrances all around," she whispered. "Sometimes it's a hole in the ground, sometimes people fall into pictures, but most times it's a door.

"The door is always in an unusual place, like in the middle of the woods on the trunk of an old maple. Or on the bank of a river just hung there, floating, in mid-air. Once, I saw a door that led right into the ground. It was made of gold and had a doorknob carved from a sycamore tree.

"That was, perhaps, the strangest door I've ever seen, or maybe it was just the idea of it—the idea of walking through a gleaming, gold door down into the earth, that made it so eerie." Arian shivered and crossed her arms over her chest.

"Anyway, there are two types of doors, House, ones that shimmer and ones that are solid. The shimmering doors move in and out of view, wavering, like heat on the top of a hill. The shimmering doors are those not yet claimed—the doors that have not been opened. It's what lies behind them that gives them their shimmer. The prospect, the hopes, the dreams, of what could happen, what could be.

"And then there are the solid doors. A solid door means the person not only found their door, but that they had the courage to walk through. I don't think that happens very often, though. There are just so many variables. For instance, did you know that everyone has a door, but having a door doesn't necessarily mean you can see it?" Arian asked.

"See, you have to believe in it first—believe in the shimmer. Unfortunately, not very many people do. In fact, many people go through their entire lives with their door in front of their faces, never even knowing it's there."

Arian smiled softly at House. House nodded back at her. They were sad all of a sudden and they let their sadness move through them—then House gathered that sadness into a big ball and threw it up into the walls to save for later.

House was a pack rat. She saved every bit of sadness, every tear, every holler and every yell. She hated to let any of it go. It's what made walking inside her so special. She had heard people say she was magic, that spending time in her was like magic. Nothing magic about it at all. The only magic was that she never threw anything out. Every conversation, every snore, every meal and every bit of love that was ever felt inside her was buried deep inside her walls. So let them call her a pack rat—because what was secreted in her walls was her pension plan.

One day, she knew, she would be alone. There would be no Lena, no Arian, not even any River one day. That would be the day that she would pull her walls down around herself. And she would be rich then, richer than anyone could imagine. She would pick up each memory and spread its color wide on the table.

Arian walked over to the fridge and got out a nectarine. She took a big bite out of the juicy fruit and then walked back to House.

"It's so sad, House. You see, those people who couldn't see their doors had forgotten what it means to remember. And so, when the moment came, when the door made itself known and stood in front of them, and said 'Open me, walk through,' they were stuck, frozen in place."

"Frozen with what?" asked House.

"With the fear of remembering," answered Arian.

"It's an uncomfortable feeling," she said, shaking her head at House. "This remembering is unlike any other; it feels like a tugging, a pulling, an ache. It's demanding. It's something you *must* have. Made up of everything you have ever known to be good and true."

Arian sank back into her chair again and House watched her eyes as they became soft, like the edges of grilled cheese.

"This remembering is made up of things like summer evenings, the crack of a ball against a bat. It's putting the children to bed and sleepy voices. The smell of roasted chicken and rice on a cold Sunday afternoon.

"People need these familiar memories because they are known and safe. It's these memories that are the very footholds and handholds that they need to find their way to their door."

"Sounds exhausting," House commented to Arian.

"Yes," Arian replied. "But it's essential that they trust enough in those first memories to make it to their door and that isn't even the hard part, because once they're standing in front of their door, then comes the doubt."

"Doubt?" echoed House.

"Yes, doubt. They start to ask themselves is this the right door? Is the door the right color, is it made out of the right wood, is it on the right tree? Will it let me pass through, will I be strong enough, will what lies beyond it be something I can recognize? And there they are, standing in front of the door, torn between the familiar and the unknown. It's the familiar that has brought them here but it's the unknown that lies in front of them. They stand poised between both sides. The feeling is so intense it's exquisite."

"And it is too much," finished House.

"Precisely," said Arian. "They think if they stay there they will surely die. They can't stand it. Because in front of the door there is no left or right. No light or dark. They are neither man nor woman. The only thing that exists at that door is remembering. And the remembering is terrifying. It's ancient and it is primal. It's a million years old. It calls to them and demands their compliance, their submission."

"And they aren't willing," said House. "Are they?" Her voice was thin.

"No, most aren't. So they let go and the door falls away. And at first they are glad, they are relieved. But as they watch it go a sadness fills them, for as soon as they let it go away from them, they have a feeling it would have been okay.

"They realize that door was warm and it was real, House." Arian sat forward in her chair, "And it would have been okay."

6

She climbed far into the night. Farther than she had ever been. She climbed into a sky so full of stars she had to brush them from her face with the back of her hand. They landed on her, soft and moist and she heard them singing. They clung in clusters to her eyelashes and to her hair. The stars spoke to her then with the voices of bells. They chimed and they rang and they cooled her hot skin.

She climbed so far into the sky that she climbed out of the stars. The sky that lay low on her hips slowly lightened, changing from pure black to a mixture of colors that looked as if it were spread across the horizon with a butter knife.

Color—now she remembered color. Hot, cold, thick and wide. For she was seeing it again for the first time, and this time she not only saw it but tasted it, as well. She took great licks of the sky like it was a Popsicle and she climbed higher. She let the colors melt all over her tongue.

They had distinctly different tastes. Purple tasted like it hadn't made up its mind yet. It was sweet but tart. Blue was a sense of longing. The taste of blue was smooth and perfect and seemed just out of her reach. Green was fast and young. It was bitter yet rich, and had the texture of moss. Black was tall and regal and she had the strange feeling that she knew black. Black was cold, almost icy in her mouth, yet strangely warm and pulsing underneath her tongue.

This was a new thing for her, being able to taste color, and she liked it. Her entire body was remembering how to respond. Now, she could feel color as well as see it, she could taste it, she could *be* it. She could wade through orange rivers. Swim around pink suns.

She climbed and she climbed. Oh, how she climbed. She was daring she was beautiful she was fast. She was flying now up the ladder. Tasting so many colors, shaking the stars out of her hair, so busy remembering that she didn't even notice that the ladder was coming to an end.

Until her head hit the bottom of the door.

7

The door hung there in mid-air, floating nonchalantly at the top of the sky. It didn't even move when she banged her head so hard against it she nearly passed out. It merely began to shimmer, flickering translucently with the coyness of a young girl bobbing a curtsey, head bowed, dress spread.

It was painted the deepest purple she had ever seen. It was glossier then eggplant. It was a color as thick and rich as velvet, as dark as communion wine.

She stared at it furiously, trying to understand it. It was like seeing her body laid out in front of her, but it was some part of her body she had never seen—a part of her that was intimate and vulnerable, that would ordinarily be hidden by skin and muscle. It made her shiver. Seeing this part of herself so exposed, she felt squeamish, she wanted to run. She didn't want to see her insides, she just wanted to trust they were there. And now, she must be willing to remember.

It was a strange feeling, as though all of her was poised on the tip of her tongue. She looked at the door and realized that somewhere inside her she knew how to open that door. She felt the excitement building and saw the door begin to shimmer again, to give her glimpses of what lay beyond.

She braced her body and prepared to jump. She tensed her muscles and scrunched up her face and bent low on her knees and reached.

Nothing. Absolutely nothing. She opened her eyes and found herself still standing on the top rung of the ladder, the door glimmering in front of her. Glimmering with ease.

Now what? Now what did she do? Her thoughts went running away from her then, flying actually, but some voice inside her whispered, *don't let them get away,* and she reached out and grabbed them with her two hands before they vanished into the air.

"Come back, come back," she yelled. After grabbing them, she lined her thoughts up in front of her in neat rows. She made them stand at attention like soldiers. She impressed herself—she had never had such control over her thoughts before, never known she could command them, that she had the power to bring them back and to make them be still. She realized with a start that she had just remembered how to do that.

Yes, this was part of it. She had to take control of her thoughts, instead of letting them control her. She had to quiet her thoughts, to make them be perfectly still. She closed her eyes and she willed her thoughts quiet. Willed quiet her fear, her doubt, her excitement and her expectation. She willed quiet her trying. And in willing her thoughts quiet, she left behind all color, all taste, the distinction between left and right, of light and dark. And finally, lastly, she even gave up She, and willed herself to a place where there was nothing but will.

Will swung the door open wide and went flying through, weightless, with no effort, and floated there while the eggplant door shut again behind it. Metal slid into place. The door locked. Will had entered a new world. Will gave one last look to the closed door and turned around, instantly becoming She again, and Arian found herself face-to-face with the Ripe Berries Moon.

The colors came back first. They had to, because the Ripe Berries Moon was called that for a reason. This early August moon was the color of strawberries. It was big and red, sitting on the horizon in front of her, so red was what she tasted first, before the moon turned gold and silver as it streamed down her throat. She tasted the strawberry moon, and it was so pleasing, so clear, so unlike anything she had ever had in her mouth before that she threw back her head and howled. And the moon came pouring down.

House could feel them coming. She could smell them in the air. She knew that they were old. They had come from some place as old as the ocean. If she closed her eyes really hard and concentrated, she could even see them. Walking single file through the woods.

She couldn't see any faces, only the hands. Gnarled knuckles leaning on a walking stick. Young fingers, soft and plump, reaching into a blueberry bush for fruit. A pair of strong hands, callused and hard, digging in the ground for roots.

House heard them coming all right. She could hear their footsteps crunching over twigs and leaves. She could hear their laughter echo over the corn. There was no mistaking their destination.

House felt their intent beat through her like a drum. It was soft, very soft at first, just a tapping. House pricked her ears up and listened closely, waited for it to happen again.

House knew she was being prepared. They wanted her to know of their impending arrival, so they let her hear them, let her smell them and let her see their hands as they walked over the earth, as they walked day and night, as they walked without stopping, to the river.

She was glad they were coming. Arian needed some company. And House looked forward to it, too. It had been a long time since she was full with people.

One thing House did know, from the softness of their sounds, was that they were coming from far away. This morning the sounds had been barely discernible. She had had to strain to hear them. Now the footsteps were distinctly louder, a constant rhythm in her ears. She had no idea when they would arrive but guessed they were pretty nearly flying. It wouldn't take them long to cover the distance.

The tapping had now become a regular noise in her ears, and House didn't even have to close her eyes to see the three of them sitting down for supper in the late afternoon sun. They were playing with her, because this time they showed her their feet. One of them had feet as big as planks and wore black, scuffed, lace-up ankle boots and sat with her feet elevated on a rock. Another had comparatively small feet shod in red canvas sneakers with blue laces. She was crouched by the fire. The third had on peach silk slippers and sat with her feet tucked delicately under her, just the tips of the brocade peering out from beneath the hem of her skirt.

She heard wood crackling. She smelled pea soup heating. And she heard them laughing. They were laughing hard.

PART TWO

THEY JOURNEY FROM ACROSS THE WORLD

—They shuffle. There is a constant shuffling of their feet as they move backward to remember and forward to dream.—

1

The three of them woke the night Arian swallowed the moon. They had, however, been stirring all day long. An arm twitching, a side of the mouth turning up into a smile. Even asleep they knew she was coming. But it wasn't until they heard the sound of the purple door swinging shut and then the moon pouring down her throat, that they really woke up. Then their eyes opened. One by one, they stood up. And began to moan.

Their moaning was a kind of calling. They moaned to find one another. They moaned to be heard. For a thousand years they had been asleep, and so they moaned when they remembered what it felt like to be alive.

The one with the gnarled hands, Urd, moaned at remembering what it was like to be in an old body. She felt the stiffness in her back, the arthritis in her knuckles and a constant pain in her left temple.

Mana, the one with the feet as big as planks, moaned with remembering the work she would have to do to keep the girl fed. She moaned for the calluses on the palms of her hands that would soon develop, the soles of her feet that would harden. She moaned for the roots that would have to be dug, the firewood that would have to be carried, the food she would have to go without.

And the girl with the red sneakers, whose name was Temu, moaned simply to keep the other two company, for she liked the sounds of their moans.

Soon, their moans were rising and moving and bringing them together. They moaned and they wailed until their moans took form and became their names, and they sang each other's names into the air, calling long and loud, until the three of them found each other, and stood at the edges of the same clearing. They smiled, seeing one another's faces. It had been a long time. It was Urd who spoke first.

"Come," she said, and held out her arms. Mana and Temu walked to her toward the center of the clearing. The three of them linked hands. Both Mana and Temu were silent, waiting for Urd to speak. Urd took her time and looked at both of them slowly.

Temu remembered Urd's looks. They were never ordinary. She didn't look at your face, or your hair, or your clothes. She only looked into your eyes. It was hard sometimes to have someone look at you so hard, thought Temu. She looked at you as if she knew everything about you, as if she knew you had worn the same underwear two days in a row.

"Temu," said Urd, grinning wide, "Why, you've got blue sky coming out of your nose." Temu blushed and touched her nose.

"I do?"

Urd nodded and touched Temu's cheek with the palm of her hand. When Urd was done studying Temu, she squinted and looked up at Mana who towered a foot above her. Mana's face was a blur, so Urd squinted even more to bring it into focus. She felt a sharp pain behind her eyes.

"Urd, your glasses," reminded Mana, in a voice that was smooth and gentle.

Mana's reminder had a strange effect on Urd. The old woman's face completely changed. She stopped squinting and her eyes went soft as figs. Temu watched her in wonder, as she seemed to forget all of what made her Urd. And for a split second she looked, thought Temu, like a normal old lady, not someone who could read minds. Not someone who could see blue sky coming out of her nose.

Mana was watching Urd with a look of tenderness, the lines around her eyes all crunched up. "Right pocket," Mana whispered.

"Oh, yes," Urd whispered back. She smiled at Mana thankfully and stuck her hand into her dress pocket where the black horn-rimmed glasses lay. She put them on and as soon as they were perched on the bridge of her nose she flipped back to being the normal Urd. The one who knew everything about you by looking into your eyes.

"Dear, dear Mana," Urd said then, now that she could really see Mana's face, and the two of them reached out and grasped one another's hands. They were silent, words unspoken, but Temu knew much was being said.

She felt a little like she was intruding by watching Mana and Urd speak into each other's eyes, so she bent her head and stared at her red sneakers. She pointed her feet out like a ballerina in first position and admired their bright red color. They had white soles, and with the blue laces looked rather patriotic. It struck her that they looked funny out here in the middle of the woods. They had the same out-of-place, lost look Urd had just had on her face when she forgot about her glasses. They looked the way she was feeling.

"It's okay," she whispered to her feet. "I know how you feel."

Having been asleep for a thousand years made her feel like a pair of bright red sneakers in the middle of the woods. They were both new in a strange land. It hadn't always been a strange land, Temu thought. Once, a long time ago, she knew this earth. It was their home, but they had been asleep for so long. The earth was a thousand years older. She gasped. That would mean she was a thousand years older.

Temu stood up slowly and felt dizzy with her thoughts. That would make her 1013 years old. The blood rushed out of her head. She wanted to faint.

"It doesn't count, Temu," Urd's voice came barreling into her ears. Temu didn't have to ask what she was talking about. Urd was back to normal, reading her mind. But she added anyway, for Temu's benefit, "The thousand years, I mean."

"Why doesn't it count?" asked Temu.

"Because you woke up knowing everything you need to know," answered Urd. "You may be feeling out of place, like your sneakers there, but you are not a stranger on this earth. You will find, as we begin our journey, that you know that we are to head north and you will know where the best blueberry bushes are hidden along the way."

Urd looked up at Mana and put her hand on her arm. "Mana will know where to find the juiciest roots. She will know where there is a cave for us to rest in if it rains, and she will know where to find an elderberry tree to make us a delicious bit of wine."

Urd smiled. "And me, well, I woke up knowing that my name is Urd. I know that we were woken, that we did not wake just by chance. I know it is of the utmost importance that the three of us stay together, and I know that we journey to meet the girl who swallowed the moon."

Urd looked at Temu and waited for her last comment to register. It only took a second.

"That's what I was dreaming about right before I woke up," said Temu excitedly. Urd's words helped her to remember.

"There was a door, it was the most beautiful shade of purple, you would have loved this door, Mana, it was the color of eggplants and columbines with a bit of hyacinth thrown in!" Temu automatically spoke in adjectives of plants, flowers and vegetables because these were the things Mana knew and loved the most.

"And then there was the sound of the door opening and closing and for a moment there was nothing. Everything was still. There was no sound. But it wasn't a scary silence. It felt, actually, rather safe. Yes, it was safe and then all of sudden I saw the moon. Oh, and Mana, it was a Ripe Berries Moon, it was huge and orange-red. Then I heard her drink it. That was it, Urd, those sounds were the sounds of the moon pouring down her throat and I knew that, Urd! I knew that before I even woke up, didn't I?"

Urd nodded. "Just as I told you, Temu. You know everything you need to know already. You just have to believe that."

Temu smiled. She was pleased with herself and it showed all over her young face. She had dark brown eyes, almost black and long whispery eyelashes. Her skin was the color of tea. She was tall for her age and quite skinny. At thirteen, she was mostly ribs and feet, knobby knees and wild vermilion hair that curled into perfect long ringlets when it was humid.

She was neither pretty nor ugly, but with Temu the definition was unimportant. She simply *was*. Her face defied her legs, which defied her back, which defied her eyes. None of it went together, at least not yet. But there was a certain air of hopefulness about her appearance that led you to believe that one day it would all come together beautifully.

"So it really doesn't matter that I have been asleep for a thousand years? I haven't missed anything?" asked Temu.

Urd was scavenging. She bent down and reached into the bush. Temu saw Urd's hand move up to her mouth, and then her back became perfectly still as she chewed with deliberation and thought. When she was done, she spit out the stem of whatever she had been eating and turned around to face Mana and Temu.

"Yes, child, you haven't missed a thing. Our reason for being here doesn't change a bit with a thousand years' passing. A thousand years," Urd sniffed, "that's small-time."

Urd picked a piece of clover from between her teeth with her fingernail. "I'll tell you what's important though. . . that you wear sneakers on your feet. That these," Urd reached up to her face, "are glasses. And that Mana," Urd chuckled now, "is clomping around in army boots!"

Urd started to cackle. Temu thought Urd must have invented the word cackle. Nobody did it as well as she did. She was also in fine form, having had a thousand-year nap.

"Not very feminine, now, Mana, is it?" Urd said jokingly, teasing her. "Couldn't you be a bit more delicate and wear something like perhaps . . . these?" Urd pulled up her skirts and daintily stuck out her toe showing them the peach silk slippers.

Mana and Temu couldn't help but laugh. Nothing could be funnier then seeing Urd in peach silk slippers, because they were nothing like her. You see, Urd's physical appearance was really quite deceptive. As long as she kept her mouth shut and didn't speak, she looked as if she should be wearing peach silk slippers. She was tiny, about four feet eleven, and she couldn't have weighed more than ninety pounds. Her skin was pale and yellow, her hair on the blue edge of white, her back was curved and a little hunched. She was easily dismissed.

But ask her a question and then peer into her eyes, and the brightness that flashed back at you was blinding. Her tongue was quick and her wit was sharp. In fact, everything about Urd was sharp. There was not much about her that was soft. From her nose to her sense of humor, Urd was all angles and lines. Skinny ankles and bony wrists. She was a study in edges.

Mana, on the other hand, was so soft she had no borders. Her body seemed endless, simply there wherever you looked. There was no real way to describe what her face looked like, because it appeared to always be changing. Sometimes her chin had a dimple in it, sometimes it did not. In the morning her nose looked long and narrow, in the evening it was wide and short.

And next to Urd, Mana was a giant. Her thighs were like tree trunks and her hands were as wide as skillets. When she walked, the earth moved under her feet. It rocked and it shook with her every step. Her hair was a planet around her face and her skin was the color of a ripe plum.

Yes, Mana was not a woman you could easily overlook. But there was a certain vulnerability amidst all that bigness, for on the inside Mana was as tender as the buds of that sweet clover Urd was gumming around in her mouth. When she spoke, her voice was warm and clear like rain after lightning. Mana knew quiet, precious things. Mana made things grow. She could grow an entire meadow of flowers from one seed.

So it was for purely physical reasons, being that Mana had feet as big as planks and peach silk slippers are only made up to size seven, that Urd got the slippers and Mana got the army boots.

"Yes," muttered Urd under her breath, "I certainly was lucky to get these delightful pink slippers. . . . Now if I could only get used to calling myself Urd."

"Did you say something, Urd?" asked Mana.

"No, nothing. Nothing of any importance, anyway." Urd gave Temu a conspiratorial smile and then went back to the bushes to look for some more sweet clover.

Temu giggled and walked over to Mana who was sitting down in the middle of the clearing cross-legged. She sat down in front of her and pushed against Mana's knees with her back until Mana undid her legs and gathered her in. Temu moved into the wide open space. Mana reached down and wrapped her arms around her and rocked her for a moment. Then she leaned down and whispered, "Want me to do your hair?"

"Oh yes, please," said Temu and stretched, trying to rearrange her long, gangly limbs into a comfortable position. "I was hoping you would."

Temu loved this part. Mana's hands were huge on her head. They were cool and smooth and they knew how to do curls. They knew just what to do with the frenzied mass of wiry redness that grew wild down her back.

Mana's hands knew this frenzy well, because it was like her own.

She and Temu had the same wild, wooly hair, the only difference was the color and length. So Mana understood its texture. She understood its moods. She knew that humid weather made this hair soft, and dry air made it shiny. She knew about the tendrils of curls that would escape on misty days, opening up and snapping alive like morning glories all over Temu's forehead.

She also knew that Temu hated her curly hair because it was not straight. She knew all about the straightening irons and the sleeping on one side with the hair pulled down tight under her shoulder. She knew about the stretching, about the pulling, about the wishing for anything other than what she had. She knew Temu dreamed of soft, fluid sheets of hair, hanging straight as a barn wall down the sides of her face.

So, keeping all of this in mind, Mana began doing Temu's hair. Curls like theirs were so brilliant and vivid in their wildness that most people were afraid to touch them. But really curly hair wanted nothing more than to be touched, its wildness to be tamed by soft knowing hands that wouldn't try to change it.

So that's what Mana did; she didn't comb Temu's hair, she soothed it. She took those curls and she touched them. She touched them over and over again until Temu's hair began curling itself like red vines around her wrists and fingers.

Temu was in a semi-catatonic state, her head tilted to one side and her eyes shut.

"Oh, a little bit more, Mana," she murmured, her lips barely moving. "Please, just a little more."

Mana's hands went on soothing Temu's hair. For she knew that woolly hair like she knew her own. And she knew what to do with that frenzy.

Temu closed her eyes. Mana's hands felt so good moving in her hair. They were cool hands and Temu let her neck fall back loosely, entrusting her head to the strong, yet gentle palms. She felt strangely sleepy. She opened her eyes just a tiny bit and squinted into the bright sunlight. She saw Urd in the corner of her vision, still chewing on a piece of grass. Temu shut her eyes once more and let herself fall into the warm melting of her limbs and face.

Everything felt heavy. Her head and her legs. She tried to move an arm and found she could not. She was simply too tired, so she stopped her struggling and finally just gave into the strange sleep that seemed to be falling upon her. And the last thing she heard, as clearly as if Urd had just walked up and whispered it into her ear (but how could that be, Urd was way across the clearing, digging in the ground for roots) was the old woman's voice telling her "just relax, Temu, relax and let yourself remember who you've been . . ."

And it was as if she was falling. Falling and falling into a deeper and deeper sleep. And when she opened her eyes again she was standing by the edge of a meadow. . . and Temu began to remember.

TEMU-ONE THOUSAND YEARS AGO

The first thing Temu remembered was that they had found the meadow by accident. It was a perfect summer day. There were no clouds in the sky, and their mothers had sent them in search of fruit. They had decided to go deeper into the forest than usual, going on a tip that hidden at the bottom of a ravine near the opening of a cave grew the fattest and juiciest raspberries.

They wandered and they wandered and eventually came upon a path. It was a small, faint path, but it was a path, so they followed it. They followed it deep into the forest to places they had never seen. They started to get scared but then Temu reminded her friends that it was afternoon. The sun was bright in the sky and they wouldn't be expected back for hours. Besides, imagine their mothers' delight when they brought back the raspberries.

So they walked on. It had gotten darker as they walked farther into the forest, so when it finally began to get lighter, and the trees became sparser, they began to sing. They sang because they were happy and they sang because the sunlight told them they were winding their way out of the forest, to wherever the path was leading them. Temu was the first to reach the edge of the forest. And the first to see the meadow.

It was filled with flowers. From the edge of the forest, where she and her two friends stood, she could see layer after layer of color just piled on top of one another. Purple loosestrife, goldenrod, gladiolus, honeysuckle, asters, clethra bushes, tiger lilies and hollyhocks. The meadow was an endless swish of color, fragrance and movement.

Temu now saw herself—the way she had been a thousand years ago, and squealed in joy. Her hair had been pin straight, smooth as water. Her hair was so straight she had even had bangs and it was freshly washed and smelled like pine.

Her friends stood with her at the edge of the forest. They were the daughters of her mother's best friends, but she couldn't seem to remember their names. She watched herself standing between the two of them. And she remembered her dress.

Her mother had made it for her birthday. It was not an ordinary dress, made of cotton or burlap. It was made of sheer silks. Temu remembered her mother had waited a long time for those silks. The exquisite fabric had traveled to them from across the world, tucked safely in a small wooden chest, carried from boat to boat, all the way from Japan.

Temu's mother had made her that dress in celebration of the earth, and so it was dyed the colors of grains—rich yellows and dark browns. Temu remembered what it felt like to wear that dress, to have the silk wrap around her legs and ankles. She felt like she was the corn, swaying gracefully, regally, back and forth in the wind.

Her basket was piled high with blue grapes and fresh figs, with white cream frothing up at the top. There were perfect pears too, all golden with a blush of red, peaches and a few apricots.

The last thing she remembered was the smell of the ocean when the breeze changed direction. She and her friends turned to each other and laughed. It was too perfect, she thought, that this beautiful meadow should lead down to the sea. She couldn't wait any longer. She had to be surrounded by all this color, sound and smell. She put down her basket at the edge of the forest, lifted up her dress and she ran.

URD–ONE THOUSAND YEARS AGO

Urd sniffed. At first she could barely smell the clethra. The smell circled around the edges of the clearing, dancing in and out of her nose. The smell of clethra was sneaky, and it was in no hurry. It teased her as it came creeping in on its tiny feet.

She sighed. *Oh yes, this was how it began.* It was usually a smell that began the remembering. Sometimes it was food, a good gravy or bread baking. Sometimes it was the smell of a season, like wood burning or cold, wet snow. Once in awhile, it was the back of a closet, dust and mothballs and gray wool. But today it was the smell of flowers. And not just any old flowers. Clethra.

Clethra was always a good start. Whenever there was clethra, it told Urd that the remembering was going to be an important one, for clethra was not a smell you fooled around with. Temu was on the verge of remembering something big, and Urd knew that because of the clethra.

Clethra always spoke of things that were. It was the smell of haunting. They were sugar sweet, barely touchable, gone before you could get enough of them. These blossoms were elusive and Urd thought it appropriate that they should lead Temu into her first remembering.

Urd knew it would only be moments before she would hear the first sound, and no sooner had she given in to the smell , than she heard the girls singing.

It was a beautiful sound, she thought, those young voices, pure and clear, echoing through the forest. Urd gave herself up to the sounds, and the last thing she remembered seeing was Mana's dark fingers weaving magic through the red curls. Then she was there, looking at the backs of the three young girls as they stood at the edge of the forest, looking out over the meadow.

Urd watched them from the trees. Her back itched and her head ached. This was a very strong remembering. She scratched her back against the trunk of a huge poplar. She tried then to will away her headache, but it was too strong. She couldn't shake it.

The headache confirmed for Urd that this was her remembering, too. She always got migraines when she went into her rememberings. She settled herself in against the trunk of the tree and watched Temu.

Urd could tell, just looking at her back, that this was a girl whose mother loved her to the ends of the earth. She could tell by the way Temu held her head—high and pointed to the sky, unafraid. She held her head like someone who knows she is loved.

Urd looked beyond the girls into the meadow and saw the poppies and the daffodils and the endless sea of color. It called to her, beckoned her, an invitation beyond compare. So when Temu dropped her basket, lifted up her skirts and made ready to run, Urd's first inclination was to run with her. She wanted nothing more than to be in that meadow surrounded by all that color and those sweet smells.

Soon, however, Urd began to feel a growing anxiousness that was at first hard to uncover, because it was masked by the beauty of the flowers and swaying grass. She stayed with the anxiousness until the invitation started to feel like a demand. The pull for her to come out into the meadow was getting stronger, it was becoming large. She felt sweat start to bead up on her forehead and under her arms. She made herself take three deep breaths. It didn't help.

That meadow felt almost alive, as if it was staring at her. Urd pulled her arms up and covered her breasts. She felt naked, completely exposed. The meadow haunted her. It teased her. It made her feel sixteen again.

She flushed. She could feel her cheeks reddening. Her nipples were tender and erect against her brown cotton dress. The meadow stared at her unabashedly. It courted her. It called her name. It crooked its little finger and motioned for her to come. It was all she could do to keep herself from giving in.

But somehow, she managed to hold herself back. She grabbed the tree from behind and held on to the trunk. This did not stop the meadow from pulling at her, in fact, it made the pull even stronger. She could sense then the meadow's displeasure at her insubordination. Then she heard the sound.

At first it was barely there, almost nothing, a hum. Then it began to grow louder. Urd shook her head hard to clear out the noise and began to sing. She sang louder and louder, but it was not enough. She realized with horror that the sound was the meadow's song. It was whistling its way down the length of the field, coming for her.

Urd was terrified. All she could do was wait. The noise of its coming was huge. It was not one large voice, it was a million voices. They were screaming and wailing, moaning and lost. It was wild and loud and it came flying at her, and at the last minute, when she thought she couldn't take it anymore, when she thought her eardrums would splinter and her heart would break in two from the deafening thunder of pain, she flung her arm up and covered her eyes.

Abruptly, there was silence, perfect stillness as both she and the meadow realized at the same time that it wasn't her task to run out into the field. She was not the one being seduced. She was there merely to watch.

The meadow left her then and flew back up, over the heads of the three young girls who stood enraptured by the edge of the forest. It turned around and faced the girls, and Urd saw the eyes of the meadow go back and forth, back and forth, looking for its target, until finally its eyes fixed on Temu.

Urd sank down to her knees. Yes, she knew it for sure now.

She was the witness.

The word *witness* came out of nowhere, but it came smashing into her head and stayed there, pulsing like a giant heart. The word was violent. It was mad. It took its foot and stamped the singing into the dirt. It took its hand and ripped the corn silk gown off a young girl's body and threw it on the ground where it lay in tatters. It circled in on an abandoned basket at the edge of the woods, apricots, pears and figs, strewn and rotting on the forest floor.

She wanted to scream out and stop her. To warn her. Don't go, please don't go. Something is wrong. *Something is wronnnggggg. . .*

But she found herself mute, frozen in place, as if her body had turned into stone. She knew she could not say a word. It was not her word to say. Nothing, nothing could have stopped that young girl from running out into that meadow. It was her meadow. It was hers to take.

Temu would be standing on the edge of the forest, picking up the bottom of her dress, and running into that meadow until the end of time. Urd let her go and just watched her in silence from the trees.

Temu ran to her future. She ran into her past. And the smell of clethra then was so thick in the air it was choking.

2

Mana did not remember. She was the only one of the three who remained in the present on that first morning. She merely sat on a soft bed of pine needles and did Temu's hair, humming *Amazing Grace* to herself as she worked.

Mana was too busy concentrating on the task before her to notice that Temu and Urd were, for all practical purposes, no longer there. If she had happened to look at their faces she might have noticed that their eyes were glazed over, their mouths were a little slack.

But Mana was focusing on the girl's head in front of her. She was winding the springy curls, like small orange snakes, around her wrists. She turned her face from side to side as she worked, to give each cheek a fair time in the sun. It was medicine, this sun on her face. She contented herself with the moment.

Mana was good at doing that. She was not the kind of woman who was always wishing she were somewhere else. She was the kind of woman who took stock of her surroundings and then got to work. There were herbs to be collected, firewood to be gathered, and she needed to start thinking about a cave. It was going to rain pretty soon, and she didn't want either the child or Urd to be caught in it. If she was traveling alone it wouldn't make any difference. If it were just her, she would walk right through it.

But children catch colds. And old ladies develop rattles deep in their chests. She was large. Yes, she was very big, and she would look out for them all.

Besides, she was happiest when she had Temu in her sights. Mana had an incredible love for Temu. She thought Temu might as well be her own child. It didn't matter that her skin was black and Temu's was seven shades lighter. It didn't matter to her that she had not carried Temu in her belly for nine months. She loved her just as a mother loved her daughter.

She looked at Temu sitting there in front of her. Mana picked up her hair, which she had worked from a scratchy, wiry tangle into a mass of silky curls, and twisted it into a cord and piled it up on top of the girl's head.The nape of Temu's neck was pale from never seeing the sun.

Mana felt a tremendous flow of adrenaline shoot through her when she saw the vulnerability hidden beneath Temu's hair. She felt herself fierce and wild. She knew she would die fighting anyone who would try to hurt Temu or take her away.

Mana let down Temu's hair and pulled her close. Temu barely stirred in her arms. She was asleep, thought Mana, and she leaned her face into the girl's hair. Her hair smelled of red things, apples, strawberries and cherry licorice whips. Only a child's hair smells this way, Mana thought, as she breathed deeply.

She was so taken by the sleeping, sweetly smelling girl in her arms that it took a few minutes before she detected the odor of feces, wet and heavy in her nose, but when she did, the odor blasted through her like a fetid wind. She threw her head up and gulped the air. Her eyes darted furiously around the clearing looking for what she knew she would find. The odor was old in her. It spoke to her of pain, of danger. Mana did not even hear herself as she began to growl. Like a wild animal, she pressed the child to her chest and began to growl.

Behind the bushes, to the left of the clearing, lay a pile of shit, with green and yellow bits of hay sticking out. It lay steaming and fresh in the mid-morning air.

3

They began to walk. It would be a long journey. They were on the other side of the world from the girl who swallowed the moon. There would be forests to run in, deserts to wander, swamps to wade through and oceans to cross.

"I hope you are strong," said Urd, shaking her head as if she had lost all hope in them. "I hope you are ready." She leaned over and pinched Temu's calf.

"Owww!" said Temu loudly and slapped Urd's hand away.

"Just checking to see if you've got any muscle on those chicken legs," said Urd with her hands on her hips. She looked up at Temu. "Well, do you?"

"I'll keep up," said Temu, examining the red mark on her calf. "You don't have to worry about me. I may be young, but I'm as strong as either one of you."

She said this firmly, with conviction. She was thinking of the other Temu who was running across the meadow at this very minute. It was like finding out you had a long-lost twin sister, only this twin sister lived inside her remembering and had straight hair instead of red frizzy curls.

It gave her strength, thinking about her. It made her feel lovely and precious, strong and capable. She felt like she could do anything. A walk across the world? She could do that without even trying. For she was not alone anymore. She had found herself standing on the edge of the forest by a meadow that led straight down to the sea.

"Well, come on then," muttered Urd to Mana and Temu, "let's get to it." They had nothing with them but the clothes they wore, so they just dusted themselves off and set off into the distance. The journey had begun.

They walked miles and miles, silent in their journeying. None of them felt a need to talk. They were glad of the chance to be quiet and think.

Temu knew they were covering great distances because she remembered the hundreds of trees she saw, the rooty smell of damp moss that crept into every bit of clothing she had on and the small piles of deer scat that lay stacked in neat towers on the pine needle floor. The forest was huge, but it seemed only minutes before they were out of it and climbing the green rolling hills on the other side. But how could that be possible?

Temu began to watch her feet. They touched the ground with every step. She concentrated on the feel of her toe and heel striking the ground, and soon was aware of an ache in her thighs, a pulling in her lower back. Soon after that she started feeling the lack of support in her arches and her feet felt long and flat, as if they couldn't move another inch. Yes, now she felt like she had walked hundreds of miles, now she felt every step. She bent her head and pushed herself forward. She felt a thousand years old. She was weary, she was so weary.

"Temu, keep your eyes out in front of you. Follow me. Stop watching your feet!" bellowed Urd, who was a good fifty feet in front of her.

Temu looked up, startled at the sound of Urd's voice. There was Urd, out in front. They were climbing a steep hill now and Temu watched in amazement as Urd literally ran up the hill. The woman was at least ninety years old! How did she do it? Temu continued to watch Urd's tiny swaying body in front of her, and soon the pain in her back stopped and then the sore muscles in her thighs loosened, and finally the arches of her feet began to feel strong and jumping and soon she, too, was running up the hill. Well, moving up the hill.

Temu wasn't so sure you could call it running because she could not really feel her feet touching the ground. She wanted to look down, to look down at her feet, but something inside her told her not to. Something told her to just trust. *Just keep your eyes on the old woman in front of you. And walk.* Never had it been so easy.

She was not breathing hard as she traveled the roundness and sharp edges, the ins and outs of the earth. It was like she was flying. Like she was a giant. Every footstep covered a mile. She felt her legs grow long, felt the lovely pull and stretch of her muscles as she brought one foot down, put her weight softly on it, and lifted the other one up. To walk was pure joy.

By the end of that afternoon, they had come as far as they would for the day. They walked across one last field and found themselves at the edge of the land, standing upon long, flat, red stones that slid right down to a summer sea.

"Good work," complimented Urd, gazing intensely across the ocean."We made up some time. I believe we are right on schedule." She was looking at the position of the setting sun which was sitting like a ball of orange yarn on the blue-gray horizon.

"Doesn't that breeze feel good?" she said to Mana and Temu as she inhaled the sharp, stinging air. They were a beautiful sight, standing there on the edge of the earth in the fading orange and red light. They were three. And if you happened to see them standing there that evening there would have been no question of there being more or fewer than three. Three was the perfect number. They were perfect, each in her own way. Perfectly ordinary.

Urd was small and tiny, her white hair in wisps falling down to her shoulders. Mana was beside her, rocking on her tremendous thighs and humming. Temu was on the left, her face turned to the ocean, brilliantly red-headed in the late afternoon sun. Yes they were perfect, all together. And in their wholeness—they were perfectly extraordinary.

"She's over there, you know," said Urd, tapping her foot on the red stones.

No one had to ask who she was talking about.

"She's somewhere across that ocean. Right now, she's just finishing her dinner," Urd said, "just walking out on the porch to sit under the stars. It's a little chilly there. She will grab a blanket if she's smart."

Urd turned to Temu and Mana then and frowned. "It's not like here, you know. This 'Maine' place is cold. Better start warming your blood up." She turned back to face the ocean and went back into her dreaming.

"Can you see the moon in her belly?" Temu asked.

Urd paused a minute and looked. "Well, not really. At least not yet. But you can hear it on her. You can hear it when she speaks. The moon comes out on the ends of her sentences. It is smooth, wet and dripping. Oh, and you can see the moondust. Yes, it's there in the corners of her lips."

Urd smiled and cocked her head as if the girl was right there and she was examining her. "What a lovely sight. I haven't seen moondust in years. Her lips are silver and gold, Temu. This is how you can tell she's swallowed the moon. You can barely see it. It shows up best in the dark, and it's getting dark there now. The sky is a deep violet."

Urd's voice faded out into silence then, as the vision ended. She closed her eyes and smiled, reaching out to touch Temu's arm. "Now, about some dinner?" she asked a few minutes later. Urd reached deep into her pockets and pulled out two cans of smoky green pea soup and a long loaf of bread.

"Oh, yes," said Temu, dancing on the red stones, so happy to see the food appear from the depths of Urd's skirt. Food made everything seem okay. Food made her feel safe. And when Urd pulled supper out of her pocket it told her they had come home.

Because home was simply there when they stopped, when they were tired, when their feet just refused to move one more step. Home was a continual creation. It didn't mean walls, it didn't mean a door, it didn't even necessarily mean shelter from the rain. It just meant a little patience.

They would only have to stand there for a few minutes, as they did that summer night, look off into the distance and wait. And if they were patient, Home would slowly creep up and circle round their feet—and when they could feel it good and thick, floating around their ankles, they would bend down and gather it up in their arms.

Urd had been sad, deeply sad, since she had woken up. She had worked hard at not showing it to Mana and Temu because she knew they looked to her to lead them. She was clearly the guide. The leader. The one who knew.

It was true, after all. She did know much, but there was a reason for that. One that neither the girl nor Mana knew. Urd knew she would tell them soon, but for now she held the knowledge close to her chest—the knowledge that she had been back. Many times, actually. *She* had not been sleeping for the past one thousand years.

Urd knew where they were going, she knew the exact route. She knew which mountains to climb, which oceans to cross and how many days it would take them at their accelerated pace.

She knew about the old rocker with the blue gingham pillow that would be waiting for her when she arrived. She knew where the moon rose and where it set on an August night. And she knew how the 23rd Psalm echoed when sung from the back of House's kitchen.

She was going back! Going to see her dear old House. She wondered if House would recognize her For a moment, she wished she had come back in a young body. The things she and House could do together if she were young! But she was old. She had always been old. She couldn't remember a time when she had come back and been young.

Ah well, old age had its advantages. People tended to leave you alone when you were old. They didn't bother trying to convince you their way was right. They didn't mind if you wore bright pink hats, if your slip was hanging out or if you had long wiry hairs coming out of your chin. They expected that you smelled kind of funny and you were allowed to wear the same dress three days in a row. And the best thing of all was that they weren't afraid to talk in front of you because they assumed, for some reason, that you couldn't hear. Urd loved that one. She had gleaned many secrets from sitting still in her rocking chair, staring straight ahead into space and humming.

But, to be fair, that was old age in Lena's time. That was the only one of her lives she'd been treated that way. In all her other lives, her age was seen as a sign of great wisdom and respect. She had been revered and set apart for her many years, not ignored and laughed at. Still, Urd wondered what it would be like to be young, to be like Temu, to have beautiful, strong legs.

Urd secretly coveted Temu's legs. It was her one concession to vanity. She dreamed of having young legs, all long and smooth, lithe tendons and muscles curving gracefully into a slim ankle or a shapely knee. Urd admired Temu's legs, but she had no intention of letting the girl know it. She had such a grand time seeing Temu's eyes flash daggers at her when she told her her legs looked like a chicken's.

Urd thought of her beloved House again and smiled. She had been sending House glimpses since they had started their journey. She wanted House to know they were coming.

Urd chuckled to herself. House probably had no idea it was her. All Urd was showing House was bits and pieces of them. Their hands. Their feet. She was teasing House, having fun with her. She couldn't wait to see her face when they finally walked up the path, when House would look deep into Urd's face and see her old friend smiling back at her. When she would see Lena buried deep in the very back of Urd's eyes.

Urd sighed heavily. She was tired. It was no wonder, though, she had worked hard, and with this lifetime had finally completed the circle in her. She had gone full around. It had taken a thousand years, but she had made it. She took comfort in knowing this was her last time back, now that she had come back as Urd. For she was finally in her original form; she was the woman from whose soul all the rest of her women had been born.

She had no complaints. It had been a good thousand years, and she had had the opportunity to experience just about every aspect of being human. Urd had lived in many different cultures, on many different sides of the earth. She carried the languages of those cultures in her tissues, under the meat of her tongue. The language of the rainforest, of the mosquito coast, the voices of a hill-town in Italy.

Urd had been Japanese, she had been African, she had been Syrian, she had been Jewish. She had been Indian, Armenian, she had been Swedish, Cajun and Spanish.

It was her bones that stored the memory of race. In her clavicle lived the Eskimo people, in her vertebrae, the Native American. And in the spread of her feet, she carried the Russians.

Her ancient skin was saturated with scent, her pores leaky. All the food she had ever eaten was seeping out; she couldn't hold a thousand year's worth, anymore, in her body. Rice and beans, tortillas, yellow curry and custard. Mango, green papaya, breadfruit and yallanchi. Stuffed grape leaves, red cabbage and a fine merlot.

When there was a strong wind, Urd smelled just like a restaurant.

It wasn't surprising; she had spent much of her lifetimes around a dinner table, for this is what humans did. Even if there was no food, there was still the congregating, the gathering, and so Urd remembered the faces, the hands, the tables at which she had sat. And in the air, the spicy smell of pig roasting, the steely blue eye of a fish at the market.

Urd couldn't stop all the smells, tastes and sounds, accumulated over a thousand years of living, from coming back. It was all mixed up now, flowing together. There seemed to be no walls that separated her senses anymore, she had lived *that* much. And so she tasted streams of sound. Scent, all of a sudden, had shape, turned into circles and spheres, roots of ice green in her hand.

It was *color*, however, that she seemed to be the most stuck on. *Color* that was plaguing her, haunting her, making her sad. It had begun in a joyful way, the colors moving through her. Quickly, furiously, she tasted limes and papaya on her tongue. But she had ended up in the painful, tearing end of color. And in this place lived the memory of the colors of her skin.

She had been given every shade possible in the span of her many lifetimes, from the darkest chocolate brown to a thick mahogany. A rich, deep, burnt red to a golden raisin yellow. Pale, pale shades of pink and white. Shades of lace and of snow, with a cool beige in between.

Each time Urd returned to the earth she would awake with wonder. She couldn't wait to open her eyes to see what incredibly rich color she had been given. It was as if she had been dipped whole and naked into the riverbeds, canyons and mountains of the earth.

But what filled Urd with joy often filled others with hate. It seemed the darker she got, the worse she was treated. There was no way of hiding skin, of hiding what color you were. Skin bravely strode forth and announced what it was.

Urd wanted to cry with her thoughts. It had been a long time since the pain had come flooding back so clearly. But it had nothing to do with her skin! Urd knew this to be true. It had to do with the dark.

Oh, it was so simple, thought Urd. All of this could be stopped if only they had the courage to sit in the dark. But they didn't. They feared the dark. It was full of all the things they didn't understand, *the things that had no name*. And because the fear was so big in them, because they couldn't hold open a space in themselves for *the things that they were not*, they began to hate the dark. And they began to hate the color black. For black became a constant reminder of their fear.

That beautiful shade of night, that rich hue of molasses, thought Urd, those shades of skin never had a chance. She didn't understand it then and she still didn't understand it now. They whipped and they knifed and they left scars. It was as if they thought they could beat the darkness out.

Urd shook her head as she looked out over the ocean. The sun was just beginning to rise and the water was taking on a purplish hue, not unlike the tips of Temu's fingertips, which were stained almost exactly the same fruity color as this early morning sea, from eating blueberries and grapes.

Urd looked under the tree. She saw Temu's freckled arm hanging out from under a blanket and Mana's plum colored calf on the bright green grass.

She turned back to the water, her eyes full of water, and held her own calla-lily-hands up to the rising sun.

4

The boat was simply there when they woke up. Temu was the first to notice it, and she came screaming across the field, waving her arms wildly, to where Mana and Urd sat crouched by the fire.

"Come look, come look!" she yelled at them, her feet barely touching the ground. Temu leaned down and tugged on Mana's arm, but Mana barely moved. She was feeling large that morning, very large. Nothing could move her, especially not a little someone named Temu. Mana rolled her eyes in good humor at Urd and Urd went along with the game. She shrugged her shoulders and snapped, "Well, what is it, girl?" Her eyes were brilliant, like two tiny seas.

Temu shook her head at them and stamped her feet. Urd tried not to laugh. The girl was so excited she was beyond talking. All she could do was point and move her hands about.

"All right, all right," said Urd sighing heavily. "Let's see what this is all about," and she braced her hand against a tree trunk and slowly lifted her old body upright. Temu ran ahead, pulling Mana behind her, and Urd walked slowly behind the two of them, a bowl cupped in her hands, enjoying the sweet orange taste of tea sloshing around in her mouth.

"Well," she said when she stood on the edge of the cliff with Mana and Temu, staring at the boat that sat bobbing in the water fifty feet below them.

It was the most beautiful boat they had ever seen. The hull was made from the bark of white birch trees and was laced together with lily pad stalks. The deck was a carpet of moss, thick and cushioned, a vibrant shade of green. Three sails fluttered softly in the wind, the stunning colors of the sunrise—cantaloupe, rose and apricot—against an azure blue sky.

"So this is what we are given," said Urd. "Could be worse," she muttered as she turned around and began to walk away.

"Urd, where are you going?" asked Mana.

"To pack up. We've got an ocean to cross!" she snapped at them, the laughter curling around the edges of her words. Temu and Mana looked at each other and smiled. They grabbed each other's hands and went flying after her.

It took them only minutes to gather up their belongings and stamp out the fire, careful to leave no sign that they had been there. It was important to treat the earth with this reverence—even Temu knew this. Silently, they erased their night's stay.

The excitement they felt, however, was not at all silent. It bubbled through them and over their heads, pulling them toward the ocean they would soon cross. Mana poured Urd the last little bit of tea before wiping out the tin with her sleeve and burying it deep in her pocket.

Urd had a soft, buttery look on her face, as she motioned Temu to her and buttoned the girl's sweater right up to her neck. Then she held Temu out in front of her for inspection. She took the young chin in her old hand and turned it to the left and right, and then finally nodded her head, as if buttoning Temu's sweater had been the last thing to do before they got on the boat. She turned on her heel and started walking towards the cliff, Mana and Temu following.

"Over here," said Urd, once they had reached the edge of the rocks. Mana and Temu watched as she picked her way carefully over loose stones and then disappeared behind a large gooseberry bush, whose pinkish red fruit dangled from its branches like earrings.

Urd looked like a tiny mummy, thought Mana. She was wrapped head to toe in a brown and yellow shawl. The only thing that showed was one gnarled hand that clutched her bowl of tea and her large bird-like nose that made an impressive silhouette against the blue sky. They followed her.

"Move it, girls," came the voice from below.

They picked their way around the gooseberry bush as they had seen Urd do and found themselves standing on a smooth , polished step. Mana grabbed Temu's arm tightly, as if she thought they would fall, and they looked down and saw Urd sitting cross-legged on the deck of the boat, staring out into the water.

"Well, what are you waiting for?" she asked, her back to them. "There's a set of stairs right there in front of you, I suggest you use them. Unless, of course, you would prefer to climb down. And then there's always the diving method."

They heard Urd chuckling softly to herself as they looked below and saw the tiny set of stairs etched into the red granite of the cliffs. From where they were standing they were hardly visible. In fact, from where they were standing they could not even see the next step. Mana sensed that all they needed to do was to put a foot forward, so they did. Sure enough, there was the next step right in front of them.

Mana inhaled the air which smelled of lobsters, green and briny, shell-like. She heard Urd singing softly to herself down below. She couldn't make out the words, but it sounded like a prayer, her voice old, quavering, in the sea air. Mana admired this old woman. She was such a tiny figure sitting on the deck of that beautiful birch tree boat, the pink and pale orange sails waving like wings all around her.

And for a second then, Mana caught sight of Urd's oldness. It was something in the way she was sitting. Something in the way she held her back so straight between the sails that snapped and fluttered. Mana looked at Urd's hands and in her hands she saw the hands of every woman she had ever been. Urd was old all right. . . *Urd was ancient,* and just for a second Mana got a glimpse of *how* ancient, and it sent a shiver through her so deep that even the sun on her face couldn't stop it.

When they had reached the bottom of the stairs, Mana watched Temu hop aboard the boat. She was all legs, arms and giggles as she ran up to Urd and wrapped her arms around her neck. Urd pretended annoyance at the young girl's disturbance, swatting her away, but Temu knew better and persisted, leaning down to whisper some sweet girl secret into Urd's ear. The old hand reached around and pulled the red head next to her own in an endearing gesture that made Mana's heart pain.

"Well," said Urd, "glad you two could make it." She spun around to face them.

"Yes," said Mana, looking all around her.

The wind picked up and lifted Mana's hair off her neck. Her eyes slowly misted up. And she began to remember.

MANA-ONE THOUSAND YEARS AGO

It started with not combing her hair. Her long, beautiful hair. Always she had loved her hair. She considered it her best attribute, so she took good care of it—washing it every day with lavender and rose scented soap, letting it dry in the sun, then brushing it until it gleamed and flowed like a river down her back.

But after she stopped combing it, it quickly lost its shine. In two days it was oily and slick. She tied it back then with a piece of stiff twine. She didn't like the feel of having it fall on her face. What had been a pleasure, moving the strands of hair that the wind had blown into the gentle curve of her lips, now was torture. She did not want to bring pleasure to herself. She did not want to *feel* pleasure. Instead she wanted to kill everything about her that was about pleasure, that was about beauty. So she started with not combing her hair, and soon after that she stopped bathing.

She wiped her nose on the back of her hand and let the dirt settle in on her neck and legs. When the wind blew she smelled herself, and at first she grimaced at the sharp, stinging odors that came from under her arms, between her legs and beneath her breasts. But after awhile the smells intrigued her. She grew to like the sour, faintly sweet, hay-like smell of her unwashed body.

She stopped washing the dishes, and she stopped watering the plants. She left food out on the table, and she no longer made the beds. She stopped looking up at the stars at night and she stopped greeting the sun. She kept herself so busy—not eating, not sleeping, refusing anything that would give her pleasure or show her beauty, refusing everything that would make her feel part of the world—that it took her a while to notice the earth was dying. By then it was too late. There was no turning back.

At first she didn't realize that it was because of her. She didn't know who she was. She didn't know that because of her, the rivers flowed. That she made the flowers bloom. That because of her the lilacs smelled like candy and the forest floor was carpeted with soft, green moss. She didn't know that the corn grew and grew out of its love for her laugh, or that the rocks remained cool in the heat of summer to make her smile.

She didn't know that she was so inexorably connected to the

earth, so she didn't understand that when she refused to continue living, when she began to kill herself, that the earth would begin to die, too.

One day she looked outside her grief and anger and noticed the grass turning brown. She looked up then. It was a slow, slow movement, this picking up of her neck that seemed to take up the length of the entire field. Her neck felt so long. But she lifted her head. She lifted her eyes and saw the death all around her.

She saw death first in the flowers. And then she saw it in herself. The flowers were wilting. Her head, too heavy for her fragile neck. She saw the slow fading of their brilliant reds and oranges. The drying and scattering of her petals. The ground she walked on had became hard and was covered with frost. She bent down and tried to scratch some of the ground up with the blackened tips of her unwashed fingers. Nothing, nothing. The ground would not move. She would accept no seed. The ground had shut its doors against her. She crossed her legs and refused to take in new life.

She lifted her head completely then and looked all around her, and at last she knew who she was.

In a single instant she commanded the birds to stop singing. She left the trees bare and dry. She picked up her arm and waved it in the air and the skies turned gray, the winds turned bitter and cold. Earth blazed, caught fire and finally, lay charred and dead.

She walked then. Nothing would feed her, nothing would sustain her, but walking. She remembered that she left her house—walked out the front door and left it wide open. Left the plants without water and the cupboards filled with mice. Dust balls rolled back and forth across the kitchen floor, the windows moaned when the cold air came whistling through. She walked and she walked across the barren earth that she had created. She walked across the barren earth that she had become.

She pulled at her hair. She pulled her beautiful long hair out in clumps as she walked. She moaned, she wailed and she screamed, but still she walked. She held the withered corn in one hand, the scorched grass in the other. Frost and ice gathered on her long eyelashes and she still refused to bathe. She became black, covered in dirt.

In the end there was no sign of who she had been. None. She was unrecognizable. And finally she was free. Free to pull back her hood, to lift her head up to the gray sky and let the wind caress the white polished bones of her face and skull.

5

The wind blew once more and Mana's eyes slowly came back into focus. She saw both Temu and Urd sitting in front of her. They were blurry around the edges at first, and then slowly came clear, but the effort to really see them took everything she had. The air was thick and stiff. Moving was almost impossible. Slowly she brought her index fingers up to her temples and started rubbing.

"Got a headache do you?" asked Urd, nodding at her.

She heard Temu whisper, "How come I never got a headache?" And Urd snapping back, "You're too young to get headaches, that's why."

Mana lifted her head and looked all around her. They had set sail. There was nothing but blue sea to be seen. She turned around. Even the cliffs with the beautiful red steps had vanished.

"How long have I been gone?" she gasped.

"Well, that depends," Urd answered. "How long does it feel like you've been gone."

Mana thought about it. "Minutes."

Urd looked at her, and her face remained perfectly still.

"Well, it's been a little longer than minutes."

"How much longer?" Mana asked.

"We've been sailing for almost a day, Mana," answered Temu sympathetically. She quickly got to her feet and rushed over to put her arm around Mana's shoulders. "We were going to wait for you to come back, Mana, honest we were. But after awhile it looked like you weren't coming back anytime soon, and Urd said we had to keep moving. We were in a hurry. But we haven't taken our eyes off you the entire time. Really we haven't. Don't worry, you've been safe."

Temu led Mana over to where Urd sat.

"Here, sit down," said Temu. "The moss is thickest and the ride is smoothest here. And if you look really hard into the distance," she pointed way out in front of them, "see there, those dark, moving shapes. Those are whales!" she said triumphantly.

Mana bent her legs and half sat, half crumpled to the deck. Urd leaned forward on her hands and knees and stuck her face into Mana's. Mana wanted to move away—Urd's breath smelled like chives. But Mana's limbs felt like a baby's, clumsy and unused. It was taking all her energy just to hold her head up.

Urd finally moved away. "You'll be fine," she announced. Mana felt as though Urd had just crawled into her chest and wandered about a bit—poked at her heart with that old curled finger to make sure it was still sound.

"It was just your first time," she added.

There was silence then, as Mana slowly came back into the present. Little by little she noticed her surroundings. She saw the remains of what must have been lunch. A heel of bread, some chives and cheese. She looked up into the sky and noticed the sun was indeed making its way down the sky. She felt the quality of light change. It went from a strong, yellow beating to a champagne hue that seemed to soak right through her.

It was just what she needed. She sighed and leaned back, stretched her entire body out on the deck of the boat and stared up into the sunrise of the sails, watching the rich, silk colors flutter against the blue sky. Letting the warmth sink into her skin, feeling the soft moss like a bed underneath her.

The salty, cool smell of the sea rose to her nose. Temu asked, "Do you want me to rub your feet?" Mana nodded and she felt Temu's delight at her saying yes. The small hands were gentle, so gentle as they took off her boots and socks. Her huge feet were exposed to the air.

Mana felt a rush of embarrassment when she remembered her feet. She didn't like to show them to people for fear they would laugh, be disgusted. They were not delicate feet. Her feet were long, wide and flat. They had bunions and corns and every other possible affliction you could imagine feet having. They were sweaty, and they were well used.They probably smelled.

But Temu did not seem to notice. She held Mana's feet in her small hands as though they were jewels. Passing them back and forth, kneading and smoothing the tired skin.

With her feet in Temu's hands, Mana felt safe enough to turn around and walk back into her remembering to try to figure out what it had all meant. It was a fragmented remembering, as though she had walked in on the middle of a conversation. All she had been given to work with was the feeling of wanting to die; of a loss so great she didn't think she could live on.

She didn't know yet what she had lost. It was so frustrating, she thought, and moaned a little. It was right on the tip of her tongue, the knowing of what had come before.

"It will come when it is time," Urd interrupted her thoughts. "No need to force it. Just think of what you did remember. That's what you need to know for now."

Urd's words were a comfort, and they allowed Mana to stop trying to yank the answers out of herself. Instead, she laid down lightly on what she had seen. She pressed her head into the pain first and let it fill her. It was hard to feel that enormous pain and not know what was causing it, but she pressed on until the pain filled every part of her, until it filled her stomach and the coldness spread out into the soles of her feet. It rose up and swam in her ears, her nose, her mouth. She knew that pain inside and out, and then she became the pain. The pain that was the unwashed, unkempt woman—past the point of caring, past the point of wanting, past the point of doing anything but walking. Wandering. And searching.

Mana's eyes snapped open. Searching? She hadn't known she was searching. She hadn't known that until now. She turned her head and caught Urd staring at her. The old face nodded and then turned away toward the sky.

She had done it. An answer had come. Mana knew now that she had been searching, that her walking was not aimless. It had a reason. She walked to find something, to find *someone*. Someone who had been lost to her, who had been taken away.

Mana felt herself flood with an enormous compassion for the woman she once was, the woman who had lost so much, who stopped bathing herself, stopped caring what she looked like. The woman who left her house, her home, with the door unlocked and wide open.

She felt compassion for the woman who had the power to stop the birds from singing. Whose pain froze up the rivers and the lakes. Who removed her hood to reveal the smooth bones that were her face.

Oh, you must be true. You must be brave. You must be so brave when you are a hundred miles up in the sky, perched on a ladder the color of bones, staring at the moon which is about to pour down into your throat.

For this is the moment when you realize how extraordinary you are. This is the moment when you realize you have had, inside you the whole time, the power to still the winds and to make the snow fall. The power to bring the rain and start the wolves howling.

It is precisely at this moment that you must be brave. Exactly at this moment when you are called on to be true, for now you have discovered the truth—that you are not separate from the sky, from the moon, from the night, after all.

It all fits then. It all slides perfectly together. Those pieces, those ancient pieces have been kept apart for so long by those who dared not dream so big. By those who dared not feel so much. Those pieces, huge slabs of stone and wall, finally slide heavily and creakily into their right places, and all because of you. Because you finally came along and dared to believe you were more than what they told you you were. More than what they told you you could be.

The nerve of you, daring to speak to the stars. Daring to wear the night on your back. You disturbed them. You made them uneasy. So they named you. They called you bitch—who does she think she is? They called you narcissistic, they called you insane. When they threatened to lock you away, you took to the streets, you crouched in the dark alleyways.

You were resilient. You were born so many times. They gave you safe names—Sylvia, Harriet, Georgia, hoping you would not move beyond their names. But you fought. You fought off their names. Listen to me, you screamed, listen to me. Listen to what is important. You gave them your words, you gave them their freedom, and you gave them your colors.

You dared to swallow the moon, gather stars in your hands—you believed you were a necesssary part of it all.

Each one of you climbed this ladder. And to this cause—you devoted your life.

PART THREE

AT THE RIVER

1

Arian did not know what to do with herself. She couldn't seem to concentrate on anything. Food, sleep, even books did not help. She felt the moon slipping way down low in her belly, almost as if it, too, sensed her distraction, her inability to just *be*. But what did she expect? Did she think life would go on as usual after swallowing the moon? Had she thought she would remain unchanged?

Part of her felt an excitement she had never felt before—a sense that deep inside her something was building. It was as if all the pieces that made her who she was had been lying down, and were now all standing up.

It was so loud in there, though, that she could barely hear any one piece. It was mostly a jumble of voices, none of them clear. The one thing she could decipher, the piece that was louder than all the rest, was a small voice that kept saying to her over and over again, *something is going to happen. Get ready. Something is going to change.* It was a whisper, the barest movement of the lips, but it was real.

Arian knew this voice. She had heard it before. She had named it when she was little. She called it "the feeling." It happened when she would lie in the backyard at night, looking up at the stars, the coolness of the earth seeping in through her pants and jacket. She had always known that she was being supported, that she was being held up. Even then, she had known the ground was embracing her, that the earth she laid on was so much more than just dirt.

She would let her body fall then, back into the earth's giant lap. And safe in that warm spot, the earth would show her the wide swing of stars. She would laugh with delight and feel herself start to sway, to reel and then to fly. When at last she found the moon, hiding behind a cloud, she would send herself swimming into the enormous universe. She would go on and on, into the galaxy, flying past the sun, past Saturn and Jupiter, through the Milky Way, until she was dizzy and breathless, stunned with her connection to it all.

It had been many years since Arian had had even a whiff of "the feeling" shoot through her body, but she knew it was there now, hovering over her shoulder, just waiting for her to put it on. It was terribly disconcerting. Actually, it was making her feel quite nauseous, because she had no clue what she was supposed to do next.

Arian was trying her hardest not to let it show. She wanted to appear calm and sure, to act as if she knew exactly what she was doing and that she knew, precisely, the significance, of carrying the moon in her belly. But the truth was she had no idea whatsoever.

That morning, when House was busy cooking breakfast, she crept down to ask River her advice. Arian doubted House would notice her absence, she had seemed so preoccupied lately. She was constantly telling her to shush, as though she were listening to an important news broadcast on the radio, but that was never the case. She even told Arian to shush when it was completely silent. Maybe River would know what was going on.

Arian leaned her head over the edge of the dock. "River, River are you there?" she whispered, trying not to let House hear her. River swam up when she heard Arian's voice.

"I'm right here," she said in such a gentle, winding way that it almost made Arian cry. She collected herself and tried to remain in control. "I wanted to ask your opinion about something."

"What is it?" asked River, lapping up and down against the wooden dock.

"Well I wanted to know . . ." Arian's voice began to shake. "Well, I wanted to know what you thought swallowing the moon meant?" she said in a gush of words and pursed her lips together tightly in case they started to quiver.

River's eyes immediately moved down to Arian's stomach as if she thought the moon would make an appearance any second. Arian covered her belly self consciously with her hands. "Well, I'm not sure that I know," River finally answered. "Don't you?"

"Of course I know," snapped Arian. "I just wanted to see if you did."

River shook her head. "I was hoping you would tell me," she admitted.

River's reply made Arian feel even worse. It was just as she thought. They all expected her to know. They all thought she knew exactly what she was doing! Imagine their disappointment when she had to tell them she had no idea what it meant. She was not the chosen one. She was just some girl who swallowed the moon by accident.

Wait a minute, Arian thought. She was not imprisoned here. She had come here, she could leave. Leave this crazy place where houses and rivers had voices. Forget it ever existed, just leave it all behind! Yes, Arian plotted, that's what she would do. She would wait until it was late, until House fell asleep. She usually drifted off early, often she was asleep right after dinner.

Arian wrung her hands together, absentmindedly watching River doing cartwheels along the tiger-lily bank. Immediately she felt a rush of guilt. What a fake she was, sneaking out in the dark of night. She felt the moon sink even lower in her belly as if her fugitive thoughts had invaded her womb.

"Arian, get up here, time for breakfast," yelled House from the kitchen window.

"Come back soon," River whispered. Arian couldn't answer. River's voice sent shivers of guilt darting up her back, so she just waved her hand behind her and made her way up to the kitchen where the rich, golden smell of House's cornbread greeted her nose.

She's being awfully quiet, thought House, watching Arian out of the corner of her eye. The girl was hunched down over her plate, staring into her food, her long hair hanging down the sides of her face.

"Cat got your tongue?" House asked, picking at her teeth with a toothpick.

Arian's head flew up at the sound of House's voice. Her features were perfectly composed but her eyes were frantic. She reached over to the vase of poppies that sat on the kitchen table and ran her fingertips over the orange and red petals. The smoothness of them calmed her, and soon her eyes became focused and clear.

"I imagine that must take a lot of effort," said House, nodding at her.

"I'm guess I'm not that hungry," answered Arian, looking at her plate piled high with pancakes and sausage.

"That's not what I meant."

Arian looked up again. "Oh," she said softly, stroking the petals again, pollen, like gold dust, falling through her fingers. "What did you mean?"

"I meant trying to pretend everything is all right when it's not."

Arian raised her eyes for the first time that morning and looked into House's face. She dared not speak, she was afraid that if she opened her mouth and said just one word it would all come pouring out.

It was awfully hard not to confess when House had just handed her such an open invitation to speak, but she just couldn't. She couldn't let House down like that. She couldn't bear to see House's disappointment when she found out the truth about her, that she was not some divine being, some goddess from the sky.

Arian looked tormented, House decided. She was pretending to look out into the water, but really she was watching the girl's reflection in the window. She knew it was not time to speak, to offer comfort. Arian wasn't ready to give up what she was holding onto yet, that silly idea that she had to be divine, that House *expected* her to be divine.

House mouthed the word to herself. It was a great word. Divine. It made her want to laugh. Quickly she brought her hand up to her face to hide her smile. Arian was so young. Hopefully, she would soon realize that what she was battling wasn't House's disappointment in her, or River's, or anybody else's. It was her own disappointment in herself.

House watched Arian chewing on a piece of bacon. She was clearly unable to hide what her body was feeling. House shivered. She remembered well what it felt like — a kind of torment, a constant back and forth between ordinary and special.

It was exhausting, too. House sighed. It wasn't easy being Arian's age. Either you were out swallowing moons or sitting there like a lump, a piece of bacon hanging out of your mouth.

It happened to everyone. Even House had been through it, but she didn't like to think too much about that now. It was altogether an embarrassing experience. One that made her cringe.

It had started when she realized she could talk. At first she thought all Houses could talk. But as she grew older and had more and more inhabitants, she realized Houses could not talk. Except for her. Important little word that one was—*except*. You had to be careful when using that word to describe yourself. It almost always led to grief.

Anyway, the people that lived in her started to tell her she was special because she could talk. She liked the feeling it gave her when they told her she was special. That she was out of the ordinary, magic.

It was a slow, creeping elation going up and down her spine. A reaffirmation. After that it was only a matter of time before the whispers began inside her. The whispers that confirmed what she had always suspected about herself; *I always knew you were different. I always knew you were meant for great things.*

Those words made her bigger. Those words made her grow. She stretched and she pulled and she burst out of her original walls, the wooden walls she had been humbly and lovingly built with. Before you could blink an eye, she had become a castle, all stone and quartz, marble and rose-covered walls.

It was marvelous being a castle, because when she was a castle, she was utterly brilliant and very important. Famous and beautiful people lived in her and her floors were always clean. Yes, House remembered she felt high-and-mighty on those castle days, full of turrets and brightly colored flags. She could almost hear the herald of trumpets now . . . and all because she could talk. She was great, she was perfectly extraordinary. She was divine.

Until the next day, when her family would leave. In the silence she would hear the creaking of her foundation. Then the mice would start running across her kitchen floor. Soon, the smell of her closets would creep out, blue and green mold and musty mothballs. After that, anything that could be wrong with a house was wrong with her. She found spider webs in her eaves, leaves in her gutters and in the bright sunlight her tile showed its true colors, old and stained. Then the whispers would start again. But this time they said things like: *told you, you're nothing. I knew you would never amount to anything.* She would slink back into the farthest corner of herself and hide, hating everyone, mostly hating herself, for the plain ordinary House that she really was.

And there it was. One minute a castle, the next a shack. Somewhere inside her, though, she knew, that really she was neither. She was simply House, somewhere in between.

So it was easy for House to see exactly what Arian was going through. She had come down from swallowing the moon and was now seeing herself as quite ordinary. She might be feeling even less than ordinary, perhaps even worthless, because that's usually how the pendulum moved. Never in the comfortable middle, it was on either edge of two extremes.

"Well, Arian," said House, finally breaking the silence and swinging around to face her, "if you're not hungry, leave the table. Nothing worse than watching someone pick at the food you've worked so hard to make. Maybe you'll be hungry by lunch. Why don't you go for a walk?"

Arian looked at her, at first dumbfounded, then angry, and without a word she got up and walked outside. House started to clear the table immediately, needing to keep her hands busy, startled at her own lack of sympathy and coldness, wondering if she had been too hard on the girl. After some thought, she decided she had done just the right thing. She wasn't there to give Arian the answers. She was just there to provide her with a warm, safe place while she figured them out for herself.

Swallowing moons, Houses that could talk, it was all the same. Everybody had one thing that set them apart. The test was in how you handled your gift. All gifts were extraordinary, but the real challenge was in not mistaking the divineness of the gift for the divineness of the person. You were not the gift, you were simply the bearer of it.

Suddenly, in the middle of that thought, House heard laughter. She heard the soft sound of water against wood and the unmistakable flap of silk sails in the breeze.

The last thing Arian saw, while spying from the bedroom window, was House standing in the middle of the kitchen, a bottle of ketchup in one hand, her uneaten plate of food in the other. Seconds later, the neat little links of sausages went sliding to the floor.

Here we go again, muttered House, that tapping. It was getting to be a regular habit. Good thing the girl had left the room when she had. House didn't want to be caught in the middle of listening. She knew this tapping was meant for her only.

At first she had found the tapping exhilarating. It brought her back to the days when she never knew what would happen next. But now it was beginning to annoy her. She was much older now, and with age came common sense. Visions and tappings she just accepted as a part of life. Somebody had something to tell her and she just wished whoever it was would hurry up and get to the point, because this whole business was getting rather stale.

Besides, whoever was sending her these visions seemed to have no sense of time—at least not House's time. She was getting tapped left and right. It didn't matter where she was or what she was doing —cooking dinner or in the middle of a sentence—the tapping had no regard for what might be going on in her life at the time.

Tap, tap tap, "Okay, hold your horses, I'm not deaf!" House shouted and begrudgingly let go. She moved into the noise and let it take her. It was like parting a velvet curtain underwater, moving between the two worlds.

For a second she stood poised between the tapping and the kitchen. Strange sense that was, her body split in two, neither half fully there, as if she was blinking on and off. As she made her way in, she was aware that she was also standing still in the middle of the kitchen. If she concentrated very hard she could feel the slight bending of her wrist as the sausages plopped to the floor.

She thought briefly about picking them up—surely they would leave grease drippings on her nice, clean linoleum—but the smell of ocean that was coming to her was so pleasant and invigorating that there was no question of going back. It pulled her right in.

She saw the silk sails. They were delicious shades of summertime fruits, cantaloupes, peaches and raspberries against a pale blue sky. She gasped. The colors were incredible. She couldn't stop staring. She listened hard now for what she might be given. There were no voices yet, just the slip-slip of water against the boat and the crisp snap of the sails in a small, steady wind.

Finally she heard it again. Tap, tap. She saw the old woman's hand first, veins like ropes standing out on the back of the flesh, her fingernails clicking on the edge of the bow. House zeroed right in, homing in on that sound. No sooner had she zoomed in than she was zoomed right out again. Someone was having fun with her, because the next thing she saw was a pair of feet.

So it was back to the feet again, was it? House had to smile. Whoever this person was, she seemed to have a strange affinity for hands and feet, because that was all she'd been allowed to see. It was the army boots this time—big, black and scuffed, laced up tight to the ankle. Well, all right, she was a good sport, and liked feet.

The army boots were not alone for long. A small pair of hands with blueberry-stained fingertips crept into view and began to loosen the laces. House felt herself melt. It was a gesture soaked with gentleness. Those army boot feet were tired and weary. They lay on the deck of the boat, splayed out, the ankles loose and floppy. They looked like they had wandered the entire earth and had just laid down to rest.

Those small hands seemed to know that. They moved slowly, carefully, as if the feet might take flight at any moment. House watched as each boot was slipped off and then the hands started to peel the socks down to the ankle.

Immediately, the feet pulled back. It was a small movement, tiny really, but it was still there. House knew that movement. She knew what the feet were feeling. They were embarrassed. They were ashamed.

House was intrigued. She looked closer, wanting a better look. Those were young hands, a child's hands, the plumpness still there around the knuckles. But it was clear to House that in this case youth did not mean lack of knowing. When the feet pulled back against those child's hands, the hands completely stopped. They recognized the shame, and they just waited.

The hands were very patient, committed and loyal. They were going nowhere. They waited and waited until they determined those feet were ready, and when those plump fingers tried once again to peel a sock off, this time they were successful.

And what feet were finally revealed! Huge, gorgeous feet, the color of prunes on one side, salmon on the other. House settled back into herself and sighed. She couldn't wait to meet this one, the woman with the large feet. She felt sure she would have an immediate kinship with her, and with the child, too. You had to respect someone who was able, so young, to respond from the clear part of her heart. House had a feeling the child was not even aware of her gift yet. She sighed again, touched at the show of great love between these two. Their bond was obviously strong.

But that old woman. . . House went zoning in again on those withered hands, still annoyingly tapping their long, bluish fingernails on the wood of the bow. House shook her head. She didn't know about this one. She was not sure if she liked her at all. A tough old bird, she probably was, not easy to read like the other two. All she knew was that she was rude as all get-out, tapping House whenever she felt like it.

Out of the three, this one kept herself farthest away from House, yet at the same time there was something familiar about her. She was an odd mix of friendly and distant. House sensed she was doing this tapping with a large grin on her face, in a comfortable way, the way an old friend or sister will tease.

But beneath that grin was utter seriousness. This old woman was warning her of their arrival for a reason. It was unspoken, yes, but the message was clear—they were coming and this was no game. She was to be ready.

With that one last thought, House was tapped right out of the picture and was surprised to find she didn't want to go. She wanted to see more. She wanted to stay on that boat under that blue and green sky, fruit colored sails waving in her face.

As she felt herself coming back into the kitchen, she heard the remnants of a voice. She held on, she reached one hand back and grabbed on to that boat, because she didn't want to miss hearing that sound. She had to strain to hear it, as if it was coming from the bottom of a well.

"Look, see the whales, Mana . . . " It was a child's voice. House tried to hold on, she was dying to hear more, but that rude old woman grabbed her hand where it was hanging onto the bow of the boat and flicked it, tapping her right back into the kitchen where she found herself standing in a puddle of grease—sausages, like cat turds, all around her feet.

Arian tore herself away from the window, afraid she would be caught spying on House. Her heart felt like it had dropped to her knees. She felt utterly alone. Even House had abandoned her.

She turned around and saw River playing down by the rocks. The sight of her swimming so peacefully brought a sharp pain to Arian's side. She felt the ache blossom like a ball of cotton in her mouth and throat as she fought down the tears. She had made her decision. She was going to run, and in doing that she had sliced herself, with one neat stroke, right out of this world, the world of River and House. She no longer had a right to any of it anymore. She was leaving and taking the moon with her.

What a coward she was. What a nerve she had, stealing the moon as if it was hers to take. She was the worst kind of fake, the kind who sneaks away when no one is looking.

River noticed her up on the porch and turned around, giving her a great big wave. "Come on out, Arian!" she called. "The water's perfect." River seemed to always be at peace. What a simple life she must have, thought Arian, feeling sorry for herself. If only things were that easy for her.

River waved at her again. "Come on, Arian. Get down here!" she yelled, doing perfect back flips around the rocks. Arian was tempted. River was playing in her favorite place. The water was shallow and warm there, barely covering a sand bar. On that strip of soft yellow sand was a line of large, perfect stones, all of them round and flat.

Arian had spent yesterday afternoon perched on those rocks in her pink and white bathing suit, a straw hat on her head, her toes dug into the sun-warmed sand. River had splashed gently around her waist as the two of them gossiped away, exchanging updates about the latest beaver den upcreek and arguing about whether trout was better pan fried or grilled. It had been a wonderful day, but all of that was changed now, now that she had decided to leave.

Arian watched, with a frown on her face, as River splashed around. River was so good at letting her body reflect what she felt. She knew no other way. If she was sad, her water barely moved, just a small pulse, a tiny in and out breath. She took that sadness right in and allowed it to render her body still. When she was happy, she allowed the happiness to penetrate her body the same way, executing the perfect backflips and dives that she alone taught the fish, racing from bank to bank .

But when she was angry, that was definitely the best show. The first night Arian arrived there was a storm, and she had watched from the kitchen window as River flung herself around and around, swinging and rocking her river body from side to side like a big old skirt, up and up until it spilled like ink right over her banks.

River had scared her that night. Arian had never seen anger displayed so openly, so undisguised. The anger Arian was familiar with felt cowardly by comparison. It lived right below the surface, always waiting, always ready, but never willing to come right up. It had a distinctive smell, like iron. It was steel lingering beneath a casually spoken phrase.

River never pretended with her body to be something she was not. "Poison," she had said to Arian. "That's poison."

But Arian pretended all the time. She couldn't help it. She pretended she was not scared. She pretended she knew why she swallowed the moon. She pretended that she was never angry, that she was always happy, that she was hungry when it was suppertime, that she was full after she had eaten. She used her body as a disguise, and now she knew why—she was afraid of what her body would do if she let it.

"Are you coming, or what?" yelled River, jarring Arian out of her thoughts. "Go get your suit on," she ordered.

Arian hesitated. She knew she'd have to spend the day pretending if she was going to sneak away without anyone knowing. She pulled her body up from its slouched position, yanked her head up, opened her eyes wide and smiled.

She had used her body so many times to hide her emotions that it was second nature now. Her body conformed itself to her will. She threw her voice out into the air, full of light and breath, just as she imagined River would expect, and answered in a sugary tone, "Coming, River, I'll just go put on my suit."

She gave River a grand wave, like a passenger waving from the deck of a cruise ship. She forced that sad, heavy body of hers up from the ground where it wanted nothing more than to be left alone in a crumpled heap, curled up in a little ball wracked with tears. But Arian had no sympathy. Up, body, get up, she hissed. It's showtime.

2

House peeked out the window at River and Arian. Good, she thought, they were still down there on the rocks. She looked up at the clock on the wall. It was half past twelve already. The morning had flown by. Arian must be starving by now.

House frowned as she watched River and Arian talking quietly in the heat of the summer sun, their heads bent low as they whispered. She felt a pang of jealousy watching them, a small pluck on her heart that took her by surprise and left her mouth dry. Oh, you are just being silly, she told herself. You're the one who told her to leave. House flicked the curtain in annoyance. It was just as well River was keeping the girl occupied. She had serious work to do.

She turned away from the window, her hands on her hips, and admired the results of her morning's hard work. The floor was white and gleaming, not a patch of dirt on it anywhere. She nodded, satisfied with her effort. This afternoon she would lay down a coat of wax. House chuckled. A coat of wax. Lena would have loved that one.

Lena never did understand House's need to clean and keep things neat and in their proper places. She was a bit like a child in that way, remembered House. She would move through the rooms dropping jackets, mittens and socks wherever she felt like it. She would bring food into bed and leave the empty plates and crusts of bread on the windowsill.

It was the only true point of contention between them. No matter how many times House would ask Lena to do her share of keeping things neat and clean, it was always the same—Lena just couldn't seem to remember. House knew she didn't do it on purpose or with meanness, it was simply something that was not important to her.

House learned to follow her silently, like a cat, folding her clothes, sweeping up the food she dropped and picking up behind her. Yes, it bothered her occasionally, but she reconciled herself to it . All in all, she thought it was a small price to pay for all the joy she and Lena shared together.

The loud, pulsing silence that had been slowly creeping around in her thoughts jarred House out of her memories. It was awfully quiet, she thought. It had been three hours since she had been tapped last. She hoped she could make it through waxing the floor before the old woman yanked her back.

First on the agenda was lunch for Arian. What could she entice her with? She knew the girl didn't have much of an appetite, and to be quite honest, she didn't blame her. If House were in her shoes, ready to sneak off in the middle of the night carrying the moon fugitive in her belly, she probably wouldn't feel much like eating either. But the girl had to eat something. It was important that she keep her strength up.

House wasn't kidding when she teased Arian about eating for two. Her belly had become home for the moon—a hotel of sorts. And that meant Arian would have to start taking care of herself. She would have to act responsibly. She couldn't skip meals anymore or not take a bath for three days, nor could she keep on forcing her body to betray her feelings.

So what was it going to be? Egg salad perhaps? House grinned to herself. She was famous for her egg salad. It was settled then. She would just need some fresh herbs. House walked out onto the porch, the gentle slam of the screen door announcing her. Arian and River looked up.

"Well, hello, stranger!" shouted River, splashing about at Arian's feet. "Come join us!"

House looked down at them for the briefest of seconds, her brow deeply furrowed. "Can't!" she yelled. She was in her work mode, concentrating on her tasks. She was looking for the perfect sprig of mint for her iced tea. For all she knew, the travelers could be here tomorrow. She wouldn't put it past the old woman to try to catch her before she was ready, so just to be safe, she planned to spend the entire day and night, if necessary, to finish everything she had to do. Then she could rest.

How nice that would be, she thought with a small smile on her face. House imagined herself sitting on the porch in the old rocker, a cup of tea in one hand, watching them all do their work, running around like crazy people.

She knew that's how it would happen. It was how it always happened. House's work needed to happen before. Her work was preparation. Baking loaves of bread, freezing pots of chili, picking flowers, washing sheets and hanging them in the breeze to dry. Her job was to surround them with comfort—to hold them in her giant arms.

She knew the work they were gathering together to do would be difficult. Life work, it was, demanding and exhausting, requiring that they give everything of themselves to their particular tasks.

House had been through this before, with Lena. She knew it was vital that they have one thing during the process be consistent and steady—one place that was not in the midst of heaving and uprooting. And that place was House.

House's hard work would pay off late at night when she would make rounds and see them all sleeping peacefully, heads buried deep in their feather pillows, quilts pulled up to their chins, bellies full and hearts silvery quiet. It would all be worth it.

Getting ready, though, meant that she didn't have time right now to help Arian. House knew she was struggling, but she simply couldn't attend to both things. The girl would just have to figure things out for herself and House had faith that she could.

House stood back for a moment, looking proudly at all the lush vegetation in the herb garden. She was pleased. The year had been bountiful. Everything was thriving, bright and fragrant. The garden was so wildly full it had almost overrun its borders. There had been many generous rains that summer.

House chopped a bunch of green onions off at the bottom of their stems and then picked some willowy sprigs of dill. She loved the sweet, feathery smell of dill and was always searching for new dishes to put it in. Maybe she could turn those home fries into potato salad with sour cream and dill dressing. Now, that might make Arian eat.

"Arian, are you hungry yet?" she yelled down, leaning over the porch railing. She bit the tip off a green onion and let the warm, full taste of it slowly seep into her tongue. Oh, that sun felt good beating down on her face. She brought the mint up to her nose and inhaled deeply. It was apple mint. Perhaps she would make some sachets out of this mint. Mix it with a little lemon verbena. Put it under the pillows and in the dresser drawers.

Arian looked up at House, bringing up her arm to shade her eyes. The sun was bright, and from where she was sitting, House was nothing but a moving yellow ball with little specks of green waving from her hand. Arian thought she could hear the impatience in House's voice at her lack of appetite.

She felt like throwing up. Her stomach had been in turmoil since she had woken up, rocking and rolling around, doing somersaults and flips. It was a constant reminder that her body was no longer hers alone, that now she was two.

Arian put her hand on her belly, and to her dismay, felt a faint bulge that hadn't been there before. Her eyes grew wild and she tried not to let her fear show. This was nearly impossible. Her mouth was full and particularly expressive, as if there was a thread that went directly from her heart to her lips.

She pressed the tiny bump on her abdomen and found it was quite firm, but not solid. To her growing horror, the moon responded immediately to her touch, giving way under her fingers, moving and turning as if it were alive. In her terror, Arian's fingers were frozen. She tried to jerk her hand away, but she couldn't.

Encouraged by the warmth of Arian's hand on her belly, the moon began to collect itself. It had been lying flat in her womb until then, spread out into a small lake, conserving energy by not being its usual round shape. But Arian's touching of her belly was like a summons and the moon pulled itself into form. Arian felt it solidify and become round against the curve of her stomach. Yes, there was no mistaking it, the moon responded to Arian's touch and became a full golden ball, tugging gently at her womb.

It rocked there warm and wet against her flesh, with small bumps, little hellos, little introductions. To Arian, the feeling was not altogether unpleasant—it was quite soothing, in fact. Within seconds, she was no longer nauseous and soon found herself rather hungry, as if some part of her that had been open, raw and exposed was now being stitched up and healed. The moon seemed to know what she needed—a lullaby—so it rocked in her belly and sang its lunar song.

Arian felt herself changing as the moon sang and dove in her veins. She felt herself rising, releasing. She felt her veins running clear. Moments later, her fear and terror were gone.The moon whispered to her what she needed to know. The moon told her that she was enough just as she was.

3

Arian was sitting out on the porch, cross-legged in the green Adirondack chair. She felt small and precious. She always felt small when she sat cross-legged—something about that position made her feel like a child.

Her hair was damp and lay in waves down her back. She had just washed up in the makeshift shower that hung from the shingles on the east side of House. She loved that shower, so cleverly hidden behind a lilac tree that made an obliging towel rack. She loved showering behind the fragrant blossoms, the late day air and sun-warmed water running in rivulets down her naked body, her hands slapping at mosquitoes, her feet dancing and soapy in the mud.

A breeze caught at the nape of her neck. She shivered a bit and hugged her knees to keep warm. It was getting cold. As if in response to her shiver, House came with a quilt in her hand. "Thought you might be needing this," she said, handing the quilt to her. Arian looked at her in surprise, but House didn't notice. She was too busy peering out into the trees.

"Mmmmm," she hummed from deep in her throat. "Nights are cooling off. Fall will be here before you know it." She looked intently down the road, moving her head from side to side, as if to get a better look. Arian watched her, curious. House looked as if she was waiting for someone, as if she was expecting company.

Finally House looked down at Arian as if she had just noticed her. "You shouldn't be out here with your hair all wet," she growled, and then walked back inside.

Arian tucked the quilt House had given her around her legs and smiled. House's comment didn't bother her. Ordinarily she would have taken it as criticism, but now she was able to see it for what it really was—concern.

Arian breathed the air in deeply. She loved this time of year. Mornings arrived crisp and clear, but by ten a.m., when the sun rose up over the trees, it was "remembering weather"—weather that filled her senses so completely that it sent memories reeling through her head like home movies.

Remembering weather didn't just happen any time, it was usually at the end of summer, late August, when the air was just the right temperature. It happened when all the smells were right, when the day was just long enough and the nights were welcoming, sleepy, dark and velvet.

Arian usually remembered in unrelated fragments—little morsels of memory, tiny bites from the past. She remembered lying on her round stomach on top of the cool, cool dirt under a huge tangle of raspberry bushes; the smell of clamcakes; singing in the car; and fields filled so high with hay that she felt she could hide for entire days in the waving gold strands.

Today, Arian had remembered herself at eight. She was a small, awkward-looking child then, on the verge of ugly, with ashy knees and elbows and a rat's nest of shiny black hair turned the color of eggplant from staying out in the sun so long.

Arian twisted her hair into a loose braid, took a sip out of her glass of lemonade, then leaned back into the chair and sighed.

Yes, it had been a good day for remembering. So many summer smells—the mint House put in her lemonade, the fresh dill sprinkled on top of her potato salad, the clean scent of River on her skin and cedar shampoo in her hair. She smiled to herself in the darkening light, pleased to have the memories flashing through her head, and she settled back to watch the night come in.

She couldn't believe how relaxed and peaceful she felt. Quite a change from this morning! The agony she had felt seemed so insignificant, so silly now, because the moment she had placed her hand on her belly and felt the moon rushing to greet her like a long-lost relative, all her doubts and fears had vanished. The answer had been in front of her the whole time. All she had had to do was reach down and touch it.

Arian threw her head back and laughed. She felt the laughter deep in her body, rumbling, bubbling up to her throat and out her mouth. What a lovely feeling that was. She heard her own laughter and it made her laugh even harder. Arian clapped her hands together and whooped into the night. She felt delighted with her ability to laugh, as if it was something new, something just discovered. Her body was humming with energy. All of her senses were acute and ready.

It was amazing, this first gift from the moon. She had been given a gift, the moon had given her back her senses and it was as if she had never heard, seen, touched, smelled or tasted until now. Now, each sense was intensified, amplified, taken to its most extreme level.

This level was loud, it was vibrant, beating with color and depth. Arian had spent hours just staring at, what before, would have seemed ordinary—like the moss on a stone.

She had felt the life in the moss— moving, soft, spongy stuff that had a voice of comfort, rich and gravelly. Its smell was simple, a combination of water, rock and earth.

Sitting with the moss relaxed Arian. She was able to move into its space and become slow and creeping, soft and receptive, varying shades of green. When she finally left the patch of moss, she found herself walking as she imagined the moss would—quietly, barely breathing, taking in only the air she needed.

Her hearing was also affected. Her acuity was increased and she heard sounds, voices she hadn't known existed. She had never before heard a rock speak, nor the trees sing. The sounds around her were so varied, so full, that it felt unbearable. She had burst into tears. In the middle of the woods, where she had been walking, she fell down on her knees, sobbing.

She felt so sad, she had missed *so* much. She had lived for twenty-eight years, and not once, until now, had she heard a flower speak.

After the sadness had passed through her body, she got up and slowly turned around in a circle, her head pointed to the sky.

As she made that slow, slow circle in the clearing, robins, sparrows and doves, the hum of the grass, the wave of the trees, the wind, the flowers, the earth—all spoke to her. One at a time, they each said just one word, so as not to overwhelm her; they all called her name in a language she was hearing for the first time.

As the woods filled with the song of her name being sung in the oldest language of the earth, Arian spun around, faster and faster, her arms spread wide, her head flung back, her hair a long, black whip in the air. She became so dizzy that she collapsed again on the ground, this time her body convulsed with happiness as she laughed and laughed at the incredible sounds filling her heart and ears. She realized that all of her five senses had been affected and her heart told her that clearly these were the gifts of the moon. She loved this new way of being. She felt as if she had been living underwater, where everything had been blurred and unfocused, until now. Now it was all so brilliant that it almost hurt.

"Dinner will be ready in five minutes!" yelled House from inside.

Arian's stomach growled at the delicious smells of House's cooking drifting through the screen door.

How silly she had been, thinking that carrying the moon in her belly would mean she had to be smarter, prettier, better. If the moon had intended her to change, to become worthy of it, she would have become all those things the moment the moon slid down her throat!

But she hadn't changed one bit! She was the same person she had always been, and that should have been a plain enough sign that *she* was who the moon wanted. The moon had picked her. Just as she was.

Arian looked up into the sky. It was darkening, lavender and crimson streaks between the trees. The beauty of it sent her reeling once again, to a place where joy and sorrow had the same name, and the emotion welled over in her for about the fiftieth time that day. Once again, she was close to tears.

"Dinnerrrrrr!!" yelled House. Arian flung off the quilt and burst in through the door.

4

It was a scratching noise, House realized. That's what she was hearing, a faint scratching. She listened closer, wondering how long that noise had been in her head. She had been so busy all day that the sound could have been there for hours without her hearing it.

There it was again. She zoomed in on it. What was that noise? It sounded like something was being dragged. House flew into the sound eagerly. It had been almost an entire day since she had gotten tapped and she was damn curious to know where they were.

Scratch, scratch. She caught her breath as she realized what the scratching was—the unmistakable sound of wood against sand. They had landed.

House was greatly surprised to find herself scared. Why was she scared? She was ready—she had spent the entire day making everything perfect for their arrival, and Arian was ready as well. Why, then, was the sound of three pairs of feet climbing out of the boat making her want to throw up?

She sat in her chair and listened, hoping for some sign, some clue as to where they were, of what they were up to. But none of them spoke. She heard only the sounds of their feet, splashing through the shallow water, moving up to the beach and dragging the boat with them.

Strange that there were no words, thought House. Perhaps the old woman had warned them against speech, or maybe they didn't speak because it was the middle of the night. The one thing she did know was that they had landed and that they were very close! The question was, how close?

Now, calm down, calm down, she told herself. Don't go panicking and forget everything you've ever known. She breathed deeply, trying to remember that her keen senses were her best resources. Her patience was finally rewarded with the smell of pine trees, spicy and damp, and beneath that was the sweet scent of honeysuckle.

They were closer than she had thought possible. Given the sharp odor of the pines that were particular to the east coast of the United States, they had sailed around the world and landed right on target —the shores of the Maine coast. At the rate they were traveling they would surely be here by morning. She couldn't stand not knowing who they were! She stood up in her chair.

"Old woman—show yourself to me!" she bellowed into the vision in front of her, her voice a giant echo in the night.

At first she saw nothing. The night was dark, there was no moon, only the brightness of the stars, and House could see that the three of them stood at the edge of a pine forest. She could just make out the feathery low branches of a blue spruce, and on the ground, at the tree's roots, the faint remnants of a path.

Then she heard the old woman laugh. It was not a mean laugh, it was just a small tee-hee—a little chuckle that made House's hair stand on end. Then complete silence.

The crunching began next, the distinctive sound of three pairs of feet walking on the dry, orange needles of the forest floor. House sighed, knowing she was just going to have to be patient. She would probably hear nothing but this crunching, louder and louder, until they arrived tomorrow morning—probably right in time for breakfast .

She supposed she should be grateful that the old woman had given her any hints at all of their coming, but right now she just felt nervous and annoyed that she had not been let in on more of the secret.

She was too annoyed to reach way behind the eaves, above the kitchen sink , where she kept all of Lena's laughter squirreled away; too nervous to pull down that indigo blue stuff, spread it wide on the table and remember who Lena was. . .

PART FOUR

THEY JOURNEY FROM ACROSS THE WORLD

1

As soon as the bottom of the boat hit sand, Urd got up and began to climb over the side.

"Be careful," warned Mana, watching the tiny old body leap over the side of the boat into the water with the agility of a young girl.

"Don't worry, I'll be fine," Urd snapped, anxious to be standing on the shores of her beloved Maine. She ran through the water, whooping and splashing, waving her arms like windmills. Temu looked at Mana and grinned, then the two of them got out of the boat and began the hard work of pulling it up on the shore under the trees, where it would be protected from the weather.

Urd spun slowly in a circle, her arms wide, taking in this coast which she hadn't set foot on in nearly a hundred years. She was not aware, as she stood on the deserted beach, that Temu and Mana were watching her from the trees.

She didn't know that her entire body was bathed in a faint golden light that came from the joy fluttering through her in tiny bird breaths. She didn't know that she was beaming as only a child can beam, and she had no idea that she was in complete disarray.

Strands of silver hair had popped out of her perfect bun and sprung into curls that lay like wet spirals on her pink cheeks. Her bony feet stuck out from beneath the tattered, wet hem of her skirt and her beautiful brocade slippers lay abandoned in the sand beside her. The top button of her shirt had fallen off, leaving the thread dangling down the front of the linen fabric and the gentle night breeze laid the shirt wide open, exposing a vulnerable patch of pale, wrinkled neck.

Urd inhaled the sweet smell of the pine trees, noisily, as if she hadn't breathed for days. Then she feasted her eyes on the pink and ivory seashells snuggled among the shiny black mussels. She walked back down to the shore and let her feet absorb the warm saltiness of the shallow tidal water. Finally, she took great swallows of the cool, seaweedy air.

Oh, it was good to be back! Urd pulled her skirt up to her knees and did a little dance on the shore in her bare feet. "I'm back, I'm back, I'm back," she sang softly to the trees.

"Urd, why are you so happy?" yelled Temu from behind the boat.

Urd stopped dancing in mid-step. Damn, those two were getting bothersome in their ability to see. It was getting so she couldn't slip anything by them.

"I'm just glad to be out of that boat," she snapped. "My stomach hasn't been right since I got on it."

Mana walked over to Urd, concern on her face. "Perhaps a cup of tea, before we begin walking then, Urd? What do you say?" asked Mana. "I'll make chamomile. It should settle your stomach quite nicely."

"That would be nice," said Urd, suddenly exhausted and feeling her ninety-plus years. She reached out and grabbed Mana's arm to steady herself. "It's okay, Urd, I'm here," said Mana softly, leaning down and nodding at her.

Urd sank to her knees in the damp sand. As she settled down, she could hear her heart beating a little too fast. She became aware of the damp, sticky sweat under her arms. She was not a child, she reminded herself, but she had just behaved as if she was. Now she was all out of breath. Composure, that's what she needed. She needed to get herself in order.

Urd became all business as she briskly wiped the sand off the soles of her feet and from between her toes. Then she grabbed her slippers and slid them on. Her hair was next. She could feel the little curls on her forehead that had escaped. That was simply not acceptable, she thought. That just would not do.

She brought her hands up to her head, a gesture she had done thousands of times in her lifetimes, always this reaching up, this smoothing, this pulling back. It gave her comfort to know some things never changed. Ancient, this movement was. This very simple movement of putting hands to hair was a woman's gesture, from the very beginning, and so, knowingly, she began touching her hair back into its usual, neat state.

Urd felt Mana's hand on her shoulder, but she still felt a bit embarrassed at her behavior, so she ignored the warmth of her palm. Instead she ran her hands down the front of her chest and noticed that the top button of her shirt had fallen off. She looked at it in dismay. She was falling apart. Suddenly, she realized that she was cold.

"I'll fix it, Urd," said Mana. "It will only take a minute." Urd looked up at her with big eyes. She felt like she was ready to drop, she was so tired. Like a child, unable to take care of herself, unable to take control, she just sat there and looked up into Mana's face.

"Here," said Mana."Take that off. I'll be done with it before you know it."

Mana reached into the bag slung across one of her shoulders, and pulled out an orange and red shawl. Now, where had that come from? wondered Urd. It was amazing what Mana held in that big bag of hers. It seemed bottomless.

Mana held the shawl up in front of her. It was a beautiful piece of work, a river of mohair and cotton threads. Urd couldn't wait to pull it on, knowing it would bring her back to herself.

Mana held it out in front of her to give Urd some privacy while she pulled her shirt over her head. Urd shivered when the night air touched her breasts, and then Mana was wrapping her tightly in the fire-colored blanket that smelled of grass.

"You just sit there, Urd," said Mana, encouraging her to be still while she and Temu worked. Urd nodded at her as they moved about. Temu was poking through the edge of the woods, gathering driftwood for a fire and Mana was rummaging through her bag for a needle and thread. Urd, feeling safe and warm, sighed under her blanket.

She looked up into the night, at the enormous spread of black, blue and purple. The evening was clear and the stars were bright —it would be a good night for traveling .

They were close now, one night's travel away. They would be there by morning, just in time for breakfast, she hoped. She didn't want to miss House's pancakes.

But they had miles to go before they could sit down at the kitchen table. Much would happen in the next few hours. Now the *three* of them would start remembering together. As soon as one memory finished, the next would begin, for they all had so much to remember before they reached her—the girl who swallowed the moon.

They would take turns moving back into their pasts as they walked steadily and quickly forward into their future. Walking, dreaming, remembering. This was what lay ahead of them on the path that Urd could see beyond the edge of the trees.

Urd shivered and Mana looked up from her sewing.

"Are you okay?"

"I'm fine, just a bit chilly."

"Temu," Mana yelled. "Let's start the fire. I think you've gathered enough wood." The girl came running over, her arms full of kindling, a rush of skinny legs, flying red hair and falling timber. She arrived at Urd's feet with a breathless giggle.

"You cold, Urd?" she asked.

"Start the fire." Urd nodded.

Temu stacked the wood into a pile. Soon, she had the fire going. As the three of them sat around it, Temu sniffed the air, a dreamy smile on her face. "Ummmm, smells like fall. Winter's coming, isn't it, Urd?"

"It certainly is. Our time is short, we must hurry," she said with a frown.

Urd could feel the pull, a constant ache in her chest. It was a yearning, an empty space wanting to be filled. The tug in her belly was strong now, stronger than it had ever been.

She could feel the strong, vital presence of the moon in the girl's belly, and Urd knew that the girl had started to absorb some of the moon's life force. She could sense Arian's wellness. It came to her in waves of calm and excitement. It rolled over her like a giant, swelling sea, and those were the waves on which she would ride from here to House's door.

Mana passed her a steaming cup of tea. Urd thanked her and held it up to her face. She stuck her nose in the fragrant, twiggy heat and breathed deeply. The steam cleared her mouth and throat and she found her voice.

"We are on the last leg of our journey," she finally said into the silence.

"I must give you a few words of advice. No matter what happens, once we enter those woods . . ." Urd pointed a gnarled finger to the trees and shook it, "do not stop walking."

Urd took another sip of her tea and wiped the edges of her

mouth with the fringes of the shawl. Temu and Mana listened silently.

"It is of great importance that we make it there by morning, or we will be too late." Urd sniffed the air. "Winter is, indeed, fast approaching, young Temu. We must finish our work while it is still summer."

"I must warn you of what is about to happen. Each of us has already begun to remember, but so far the rememberings have been infrequent, and you have been given time to rest after each one."

Urd put her mug down on the ground and took a minute to look into both Temu's and Mana's eyes. Temu looked terrified, her dark eyes wide and full of fear. Mana just looked tired, resigned to what lay ahead.

Gently Urd said, "I believe these next few hours will be full of rememberings. You will feel exhausted with the enormity of them, as if you can't go on, that you can't possibly be expected to walk one more step. You will be sleepy, you will be full of anguish, you will want nothing more than to stop. YOU MUST NOT. You must keep walking. Above all else, remember that. You are to keep walking, no matter what. Is that clear?"

Temu and Mana nodded, and Urd watched while Temu scurried next to Mana and buried her face in the woman's shoulder. Mana stroked the mass of red curls, and Temu looked out at Urd with frightened eyes.

"All right then, I don't mean to frighten you, but I think you should know what to expect. Then it won't take you by surprise. Just keep moving those feet. If you stop, you will get lost. You will lose your way and I will lose you. You must let the remembering play itself out. You must go through it to the end. If you stop somewhere along the way, if you become frozen in your terror or mourning, that is exactly where you will stay! You will fall back into the past, into the remembering and you will remain there.

"You see, that's what the remembering does. It pulls you back. You have a chance now for a new future, but you won't be ready to walk into the future until you fully embrace your past. This is your task on this journey—to face your past."

Urd snapped her head to the right and leaned into where Temu and Mana were sitting. "Are you all right?" she asked.

Temu jumped back, startled at her quick movement, and Urd

saw Mana's hand fly protectively to the girl's shoulder. They had both visibly shrunk away from her as she had spoken.

Mana spoke for both of them. "Yes, we'll be all right," she said.

"There will be pancakes and hot syrup for breakfast," Urd told them. "You can look forward to that."

"I love pancakes," said Temu, picking her head up from Mana's shoulder. "Do you think they will have blueberries in them?"

"I would think so," answered Urd. "They are in season after all."

"Don't be afraid, my little one," she said, reaching out to her in a rare show of affection, stroking the soft, freckled cheek. "You don't know your own strength yet. Soon you will."

"And you, Mana, you might be the bravest of all. Now, is my shirt done yet?" she asked, eyeing the pile of linen sitting in Mana's lap.

"Yes, it is," Mana handed it back to her.

"Good," she said and slowly stood up. She stood in front of the fire, her vision lost in the flames. Then, as if she had forgotten Temu and Mana, she let the shawl slip from her shoulders and she stood there exposed, large breasts hanging low on her distended stomach, her arms all loose skin and goose bumps in the evening breeze.

Temu and Mana stared at her. They couldn't help it. Her old body compelled them. They took it all in, the skin that slipped like a soft white river, pouring gently down her chest, the pink nipples, the faint line of hair that ran from her belly to the elastic waist of her skirt.

Then to their surprise, she touched herself. She reached up and cupped her left breast. She pulled it up high on her chest, where it might have sat seventy years ago, and she looked down at it and smiled, her lips curled up sweetly.

"I used to have beautiful breasts, you know." Her eyes were moist and glazed. Then slowly, slowly, as if she was parting from it forever, she let her breast fall and it slid gently back down to the curve of her belly. She watched it sink into place beside the other and she sighed. Then, as if it was the last thing in the world she wanted to do, she pulled on her linen shirt, making sure it was buttoned up to her neck.

Then she turned to Temu and Mana and gave them a smile.

"Shall we go?"

2

MANA

The woods were dark. Deep, deep green and black. In some places Mana could barely see the trail, but her feet knew where to go. She was scared—terrified. The smell of shit was all around her. It had been circling her for some time now, darting in and out of the trees, flying low at her feet and high above her head.

Now it had gotten worse, for it was all around her face. Like some long, sleek animal, the faintly sweet smell of shit had crept onto her head when she wasn't looking and now it had its claws deeply embedded in her wild mane of hair. She could hear it laughing as it draped itself over her forehead like a mink and hung low over her eyes. With every step she took it bounced right in her nostrils.

She tried slapping the smell away, waving it out of her face, but she could feel it, dark and heavy, languishing, grinning, from its resting place on her head.

She forced herself to keep walking. The faster she got there the sooner this would be over. She fought down the smell, but it was intoxicating, alluring. It reeled her in. She could not stop it—this was her remembering—so she followed the smell right down to the ground, to a place where the earth had been split wide open.

But by the time Mana came riding on the furred back of her remembering, all that was left of the earth's great heaving open were ten steaming piles of horseshit that lay scattered in the middle of the meadow in a jagged line.

This was the only marker, the only evidence that the earth had been ripped open. This and the echo of her daughter's screams.

Keep walking, keep walking, she told herself. She stomped through the woods, making her steps hard and heavy, making her steps count. She reached out and touched the branches of the trees as she sped by. Get me through here, she prayed. Just get me through here. She felt the sweat running down her forehead, she felt the ache in the front of her thighs. She walked on. She walked on. She walked deeper.

Her daughter's screams lay muffled and buried in the trunks of the trees, but the trees did not speak. For they had been warned—they had been threatened—*your silence or your life.*

So the trees did not tell her. They were silent when Mana threw her head up to the sky and wailed. They were silent when she pounded the ground with her fists, when she crushed the hyacinths under her feet to a blood-purple pulp. They were silent when she thrust her hands into the piles of horse shit and smeared the yellow-brown stuff on her face and breasts.

When the anguish of her cries beat through them like hundreds of tiny axes, the trees finally broke, for her cries tore their hearts apart and they began to drop their leaves—healthy, green leaves that had not been shed for thousands of years. As the leaves fell through the air they changed color from green and yellow to orange and red. They bled through the bright blue sky until the branches were bare.

But Mana was in far too much pain to see the sign the trees had given her. Searing, not-to-be-believed pain. She knew she could do nothing to stop it, so she sat and endured it. Head bent, shoulders slumped, covered in horse shit, she let the pain rock through her. She was shuddering violently. Her arms flew up to cover her face as the tidal wave of pain flowed over and into her body, not missing one cell, one little atom. The pain did not leave until it was sure it had touched all of her.

And when it was done, Mana lay curled on the ground. Her clothes were torn, her arms and legs were bleeding. She remained there for awhile, frozen, unable to convince her limbs to move until she became aware of a strange noise coming from beneath her dress.

Mana slowly picked herself up and backed away. She saw a perfect circle of crushed daffodils and green grass. Mana looked closer, and then she smelled it—the scent of smoke. The patch of grass was burning. She watched in horror as the grass she had been sitting on began to smoke, crisping and then sizzling. Seconds later it was brown and dead.

Her hand flew to her mouth, her eyes wide with fear. She backed slowly away from the clearing. And then she was running.

She could hear the fire chasing her. It was right behind her, licking at her heels. She covered her ears and she ran, the sound of the burning earth thundering in her head. The burning was so loud, so loud, that she didn't hear the muffled tapping beneath her feet. She didn't hear the tapping that followed her as she ran—the sound of her daughter's fists beating through the miles of earth under which she was buried.

"Mother, Motherrrr !" her daughter screamed. "Help me. . . !"

Mana heard nothing.

Mana walked on.

3

Urd looked down at her feet and smiled, amazed at her progress. She was moving along at quite a good speed. Not bad for an old woman, she thought. She looked in front of her and watched young Temu for awhile. She was obviously not in a remembering yet, for Urd could see her popping blueberries into her mouth, her red curls swinging down her back. Urd shook her head—that girl had a huge appetite for such a skinny little thing. She always seemed to be eating something.

Mana, however, was a different story. Urd didn't even have to turn around to know she was deep in her remembering already. She could feel Mana's grief and pain washing against her back and shoulders like a black wave.

And she could smell Mana's remembering—a wall of shit pushing against the back of her calves. She decided to give Mana a little encouragement, a reminder of where she was.

"Mana, Mana!" Urd whispered. "Don't forget, keep walking!"

Urd waited for a moment to hear Mana's reply in her head, but she heard only a strange crisping sound. She tried again, this time a little louder. "Mana, can you hear me? Answer me if you can!" Nothing. The crisping noise grew louder.

Damn! Mana was sinking into her remembering, her pain so great she was no longer moving in this world. She had stopped walking into the future, and was, instead, running like a madwoman back into the past.

Without thinking about the consequences, Urd turned and faced that black wave of pain and dove right in. She dove into the deepest darkness of Mana's remembering and found herself stuck in the tar-like entrance to Mana's past.

Now this was a surprise! She had expected to dive in and come right up on the other side, an easy entrance. Urd had imagined Mana's pain to be sleek and slippery because she had seen Mana slide right in.

But the way in now was as thick as molasses, and Urd realized that her arrival was not welcome at all. The smell that had lured Mana in had solidified into a wall, making it nearly impossible for Urd to break through. She could barely move, barely breath. Just when she began to fear she might suffocate, she heard a voice—the faint cry of a young girl—and then she heard the beating of fists on solid earth. That was all the fuel she needed.

She grabbed onto that sound and wrapped it around her waist, tying it into a firm knot, then proceeded to pull herself in. She reeled herself right through that wall of pain with a strength she hadn't known she had and popped like a champagne cork out of the dark stench of Mana's remembering to find herself ten feet off the ground in the wide branches of a poplar tree.

Off in the distance she saw a woman running, tearing the hair from her scalp as she ran. She was trying desperately to outrun the burning grass that licked her ankles, scorching a wide black path behind her.

4

TEMU

Temu was eating blueberries as fat and plump as her thumbs and walking like a giant through the woods. She loved this kind of traveling. She never felt tired. Her feet barely touched the ground. It was a little like flying, she thought. Her feet just took care of themselves. All she had to do was lift her arms out from the sides of her body like wings and brush them against the bushes and the fruit just fell into her waiting hands. Oh, she liked this Maine place. Never had she seen so many luscious berries, and they were so fragrant too—the very smell of summer. She began to hum. She turned around to make sure Urd was there. Sure enough she was, muttering to herself as usual, her eyes down, looking at the ground.

Temu continued walking, then she began to skip.

This was easy, she thought. What was so hard or dangerous about this? How could anything bad happen when the woods smelled so sweetly of pine and cedar and she was eating blueberries the size of grapes!

Soon they would be there! Soon she would meet the girl who swallowed the moon, and they would have pancakes for breakfast and maybe a swim later in the morning. She couldn't wait, she just couldn't wait. She began to walk even faster, then she began to run, thinking that the sooner she got there the sooner she could eat.

She ran until the first wave of flowers hit her and stopped her dead in her tracks.

5

MANA

Mana ran, and she ran with a faint remembrance, like an itch, in her head. She was forgetting something, but the more she ran, the fainter the itch became, and soon it disappeared altogether. The sizzling of the burning grass took its place.

When she ran, her body thundered on the earth beneath her. She ran like a buffalo, angry and wild, large clumps of earth spitting up from beneath her bare feet. No sooner had she managed to clean out a tiny space for herself into which she had every intention of crawling to hide from the pain, than the word STOP screamed into her head, in such a commanding voice that Mana did just that.

Suddenly she was still. Her hair came whipping around her face, then slid back into place. The breeze died. All was silent. Slowly, she turned and looked back to where she had been and saw the old woman sitting daintily in a tree.

She saw her in utter detail, sitting on a branch, swinging her legs fearlessly back and forth. She looked as if she had been sitting in that tree all her life.

When Urd saw that Mana had turned around, the old woman gave a little wave, raised one eyebrow and began to make small clucking noises. Mana stared at her. The old woman looked crazy —she looked nuts—she had eyes that were the color of the sun.

LISTEN, the old woman commanded her without sound. LISTEN. And when Mana blinked her eyes and looked again, Urd was gone.

❖ ❖ ❖

Urd barely missed a step as she returned to her own walking, sliding into her peach slippers, which she found waiting for her about fifty yards ahead of where she had left them. She arrived just in time to see Temu begin to run down the path in front of her.

Oh dear, she thought, one right after another. But there was no turning back; there was nothing to do but keep moving.

"Good luck, my little Temu," Urd whispered, watching the red curls bouncing on the girl's shoulders as she leaped, her long, beautiful legs carrying her off into the darkness. "Good luck."

Urd knew that Temu would find herself exactly where she had left during her last remembering—on the edge of the clearing, looking out into a meadow filled with flowers. In a minute, Temu would be abandoning her basket, picking up the soft edges of her silk dress and running into that meadow like there was no tomorrow.

6

TEMU

The meadow was such a rushing river of color that it hardly looked real. It hurt Temu's eyes to look at it. She felt blinded by its intensity, but there was no turning away—she was riveted.

Temu reached up under her hair where her neck was damp. She brought her fingers up to her nose and sniffed. Her sweat smelled like metal, like iron.

She drew her attention back to the meadow and breathed deeply. She felt a sense of awe flutter through her. She let it rise and fall, spin and rush, until it exploded into tiny gold sparks inside her.

"Oh, thank you," she prayed, under her breath, gathering the sparks and pulling them down into her feet where she sent them shooting into the earth from the very tips of her toes. Before her was every shade of pink, from the palest, softest rose to the most shocking fuchsia. There were purples and lavenders, indigos and delicate violets. There were reds—crimson and brick, ruby and apple. Yellow was interspersed throughout, butter and sun, egg yolk and mustard. And then there was blue. Blue so rich it made her soul ache.

She heard a tiny voice then, deep in her ears. An old voice, a very old voice. "Don't forget to keep walkingggg. . ." she thought it said. But it faded, and in its place was color—pulsing through her, surrounding her, intoxicating her, willing her to move. Finally she did. Finally she ran. She pulled those beautiful long legs of hers underneath her and she ran, whooping and screaming with delight, into that meadow.

She began to sing, and as her young voice floated up into the air, the honeysuckle and the poppies, the snapdragons and sunflowers, picked up their heads and began to grow. Her voice was like water. She made the flowers grow.

A forest now. *A forest we will become.* Like brothers and sisters, the flowers helped each other to the sky. And once they were well up into the blueness, they bent their fragile necks towards the girl and wrapped their soft, fragrant arms around her, drawing her attention to the sweetest, most beautiful blossom of them all.

Pick it, pick it, they whispered.

Pluck it, pluck it, it is yours.

This one? she asked with a smile.

Are you sure this is the one?

Yes, they nodded, kissing her hands and feet with their sweet hyacinth breath.

That is most certainly the one.

It was, she thought, the most beautiful flower she had ever seen. It was in the peak of blooming, each delicate layer of petal beating out towards the sun. It looked very old, this flower, ancient, yet she knew this couldn't be so. It had a wet heady perfume that told her it had bloomed just hours ago. Still, somehow, it looked old, with a strange violet light pulsing around it.

It seemed strange that she did not know what kind of flower it was. Temu thought she knew the name of every flower. She had become an expert on growing things. Her mother had spent weeks, months, out in the fields and woods with her. Together they had gathered herbs, flowers and seeds. They would come home late in the day with their baskets piled with sweet-smelling lavender and sage. Later, after dusk, she and her mother would sit on the front steps of their house, surrounded by bowls and dishes of multicolored petals and stems. Her mother would sing as she twisted and crushed and ground the different colors and smells together.

Yes, she decided, her mother would be delighted by this blossom. It was the color of a wedding dress, as delicate and fragile as lace. Temu would pick it and take it back as a present. She wrapped her young hands around the thick, wet stalk and plucked the biggest white bloom she had ever seen.

Seconds later, she was gone.

There were no words to describe what the earth sounded like when it split wide open. For contrary to what Urd thought the sound of the earth's ribcage being cracked in two would be—harps, bells, thunder—she was wrong. It was not deafening. And it was not beautiful. It was, in fact, the sound of nothing.

Urd wanted to name that sound. She had been on this earth many times—she was the one who had stood at the crossroads of time when time began. The name of the sound was dancing on the tip of her tongue. Somewhere, within her, she knew its name.

She dug deep in her knowing, scrounged around in the back drawers of her memory, flinging visions and scenes from all of her lives here and there, and finally she found the scrap of familiarity she was looking for.

She picked up that piece of memory and held it up to the light. It was *unsound*—a sound so black, so bottomless that it drew all other sound into it. The rich velvet silence was all encompassing, all knowing—and undeniable.

Urd watched as the *unsound*, like a transparent thousand-ton weight, blanketed itself upon the meadow, the flowers and the young girl, pushing them, pulling them all down into the crack of the earth.

Temu slid in feet first, a look of surprise on her face. At the last minute she grabbed onto the stems of two flowers, as if to keep herself above ground, but she continued to be sucked in, her hands smeared orange with pollen, a few stray seeds stuck to her wrist. The last thing Temu saw before the earth closed up tight like a seam, were the glistening black hoofs of a horse rearing up on its hind legs.

Then the *unsound* lifted.

And the screaming began.

7

DEMETER

Mana did as the old woman in the tree commanded her—she listened. But she was too far away to hear her daughter's fists. All she heard was a vast silence that spread like a continent before her.

Mana felt herself being swept away by this silence, a silence that rose and became deafening in her ears. A silence so loud and devoid of air, that she didn't hear the sound of the beast's footsteps as it approached her.

So she had no warning when the beast grabbed her by the hair and bared her neck. When the beast bent to rip her throat wide open with one smooth sweep of its powerful jaws.

There was nothing Mana could do about it. The beast was very strong. And if truth be told, there was some part of her that enjoyed the feeling of her head in the giant hand. She liked the feeling of her throat laid bare, of the breath on her neck, hot and steaming and hard.

"Demeter," the beast named her as she had once walked the earth. "Demeter."

The sounds of the beast reclaiming its own.

8

TEMU

At first she just screamed—an eye-piercing scream—because swimming in the dirt in front of her, two inches from her face, were the things of which nightmares are made.

Black, hairy spiders scuttled around her hairline, pausing to look at her with their bulbous eyes, their furry legs tapping against her forehead. Long, wet, pink worms, healthy and plump, draped themselves over the shells of her ears. She could smell them. They smelled like water and rain, unthreatening, but she couldn't bear the damp coolness of them next to her unprotected head.

There were rats—creatures with scapel-thin lips and agate eyes. They burrowed up to her and wrapped their muscular bodies around her neck like scarves, their hairy snouts moving from side to side as they sniffed her skin. Finally they settled into the curve of her neck, mesmerized by the wild pumping of blood through her jugular.

Temu screamed. She was going to die! She had been buried alive and these wretched creatures would surely kill her !

She began pounding her fists on the earth wall above her. "Mother, Motherrrr," she screamed. "Save me! Mother, help me, I'm dying. I'm dying!" But her screams were muffled by the tons of dirt under which she lay.

On the surface, her screams produced only a mere shaking of the flowers. Her mother was there, above her, but was running for her life as the meadow burned up under her feet, and she could not stop and hear her daughter's screams.

Someone did hear Temu's screams though—someone who was underground. And to him, the girl's screams rang out joyously, like music, for he had been awaiting her arrival for what seemed like forever, deep down in his home in the belly of the planet.

He smiled when he heard the young girl scream. "My beloved, you've finally come," he whispered, his eyes shining in the darkness, his voice a brilliant silver.

"Oh, but you're so scared. . ." he said, aware that his gentle whisper would travel upwards as clearly as her screams traveled down, and seconds later his words arrived in Temu's ears.

Temu heard the compassion in his voice, and she immediately stopped screaming. There was somebody down there who had a voice like an orchestra, all flutes, harps and strings. The voice spoke to her of protection, it spoke of comfort and strength, but Temu also detected an anxiousness, a forwardness that she couldn't quite decipher. She realized that the voice also seemed to have an effect on the creatures draped all over her. As soon as the voice uttered its first word, the spiders began to fall from her forehead, the worms wriggled off her ears and the rats crawled back into their tunnels.

"They are not trying to hurt you," the voice told her. "They are just curious. But for now, until you get to know them, I will keep them from you." And the voice held her face gently in its hands.

"Now, are you ready? Are you ready to come down?" the voice asked. Temu nodded hesitantly. She was afraid of the voice. It seemed to be constantly changing—one second it sounded like a beloved song, the next it was the sound of a robin's egg dropping out of its nest.

She realized, though, that she was more frightened of staying where she was than of meeting the owner of the voice. She didn't care if the worms and mice were friendly and merely curious. She just couldn't bear to be alone in the dark.

So she whispered. "Yes, I'm ready to come down."

"Very well, my love," the voice answered. "You don't know how long I've waited to hear those words."

And she began her descent.

9

PERSEPHONE

He pulled her down by her feet, into the rich, black soil. His pull was insistent, his fingers firm around her delicate ankles, and she knew he would not let go. Her palms were sweating, her skin felt tight. She was cold and hot, she shivered and felt her nipples stiffen.

Without thinking about it, she pointed her toes as he pulled her down to him, aware that her feet were one of her best features. She had beautiful arches and smooth unblemished heels.

Her heart was pounding inside her chest. She smoothed her hair back from her face and dared to look down, to see who was pulling her into the depths of the earth.

The hand that was attached to her foot was large and warm and strong. She saw a wide palm, long, tapered fingers, and a substantial river of hair that grew down the arm and wrist. The hair made Temu gasp. It embarrassed her and it excited her. She began to sweat and shiver again.

"I'm not scared, I'm not scared. . ." she chanted to herself, realizing it was true. She had never felt more alive, more awake than in those moments when a stranger's hand pulled her down to the center of the earth.

She traveled down for miles. The dirt around her became darker and darker. The worms disappeared, the bugs vanished, until there was nothing but pure, clean loam and then the smell of water. When she felt it couldn't possibly get any blacker, suddenly it began to get light again. It was then that she heard him laugh, felt his soft breath on her calves, whispering up her skirt. Seconds later she was standing in front of the most beautiful man she had ever seen in her life.

He smiled at her with eyes the color of the sea.

"Persephone," he called her, with a voice like crushed rose petals.

She fainted dead away.

PART FIVE

THEY MEET AT THE RIVER

1

Both Arian and House cried the morning that Temu, Mana and Urd finally arrived. They cried for different reasons, though.

Arian cried when she saw the sun rising from the roots of the purple night trees, because now she knew the delicious warmth they were feeling on the backs of their trunks. House cried because she was so tired. She had been up all night, not finishing her work until the sun rose. She was ready to drop.

So the two of them had themselves a good cry out there on the porch, until the sun got caught in the branches of the big oak tree across River. Then House got up slowly, one hand on her aching back, and quietly went into the kitchen to start breakfast.

All night, House had heard them coming. It had been a rough night for them, she knew. They would be exhausted when they arrived. They would want breakfast and then they would probably fall right into bed. House was ready—she had everything planned.

The child and the woman with the army boots would share the biggest of the three bedrooms, the one that looked out on River. It was a large, pleasant room, the walls a pale green, with a slanted wooden floor. There was one large bed in there, big enough for two, and House had pulled down extra feather pillows from the closet. The bed was piled high with quilts and comforters, all lace and different shades of white. The sheets were freshly washed and the room smelled of lemon and cedar. There was a vase of asters and lilies on each of the bedside tables and a large bowl of oranges on the desk. House had even found two nightgowns. She wasn't sure they would fit, but she put them, neatly folded, on the bed.

House shut the door to what would be Mana and Temu's room and walked into the other bedroom. This was where the old woman would sleep. It was a small bedroom, the smallest of the three in the house. It had been Lena's bedroom, she had always liked it best. House had thought she was crazy, the porch bedroom was really the nicest, but Lena had always been partial to the smallest room that was tucked away in the corner of House.

It was a room filled with memories. House didn't go into it often now; it was hard to be in there and not miss Lena. On the few days when she had gone in to give the room a light dusting, or open up the window when spring came, House had ended up spending the entire day in there. The room was filled with Lena—her possessions, her spirit.

But yesterday, when House walked in to clean, she found the room strangely quiet, devoid of memories. It felt as if the room were holding its breath, as if it was waiting.

The room had a wide, long window on its west side that opened out onto the herb garden. When they had first landed at River's foot, Lena had slid her bed from the middle of the room, where it had always been, to right under that window and she had never moved it again.

She loved to fall asleep with the evening breeze in her face, the smell of wet grass and rocky soil creeping in, lulling her to sleep. She said the smells of the night sent her off into good dreams, and Lena was always in search of good dreams. Even in winter the window would be open, her small body covered in piles of blankets and comforters, her face turned toward the glass panes, as if she was expecting someone to come through.

"The night air is my lover," she used to tell House. "I am too old to have any other kind, and it's important to always have a lover. You must always leave yourself open to love, and when you get to be my age, the lovers that come courting have the strangest faces. At first you question those faces. 'Wait,' you say, 'this is not what I remembered. This is not what love looks like.' But after a while, you realize that love does not look just one certain way, and so you open the window, you let the night air in. Because that air has become a lover who touches your skin as tenderly as if it was the softest thing imaginable."

And so, no matter what the weather, when Lena had been alive, the window had always stayed open.

House shut Lena's door and walked back into the kitchen. She heard a splash. Arian was taking her morning swim. House looked at the clock. It wasn't even six yet. It was going to be a long day. She reached into the cupboard and pulled out her big mixing bowl. She was making a double batch of pancake batter.

House leaned out the window. "Arian, pick me some of those blueberries!" Arian turned around, treading water.

"Pancakes?" she asked. House nodded at her through the screen. Arian paddled over to the shore where the blueberry bushes grew.

House got out the eggs and flour and began to mix up the recipe she knew by heart. She threw in a splash of vanilla, a sprinkle of nutmeg and took a quick look out the back window at the dirt road. Nothing so far, but they were close. She could hear their footsteps like her heartbeat. They were right around the corner.

She walked out on the porch. "Arian, I need those blueberries now!" Arian turned around from where she stood knee deep in water. House could see the gold of the moon streaming in little currents right beneath the surface of her brown skin.

"Okay, okay! I didn't realize you were in such a hurry!"

She swam back across River holding a silver pail of blueberries on her head. "Here," she said, handing them to House. "There's tons of them over there. I just had to shake the bushes, I didn't even have to pick them." House took the pail from her and handed her a towel.

"Dry off and get dressed."

Arian looked at her quizzically. "Why, what's the hurry?" she asked.

"Just do it, Arian, I don't have time to explain." House sighed heavily.

"House, are you all right? You look exhausted." Arian wrapped the towel around herself and tucked the edges of it up around her breasts. "Didn't you sleep well last night?"

The concern in Arian's voice made House want to cry. House thought she should feel exhilarated at the excitement that was about to happen, but instead, she found herself feeling sad that it would no longer be just the three of them—House, River and the girl who swallowed the moon.

"Oh, enough of this foolishness!" House said, "I've got work to do. Breakfast will be ready in fifteen minutes. You can go back and finish your swim if you want."

"You don't mind? I could come in and help."

"No, I'm fine. Look, River is waiting. You go ahead."

"Okay, then." Arian shrugged, threw off her towel and jumped into the water.

House went back inside and dumped the berries into the batter. She gave the mixture one good stir and then poured eight perfect circles on the sizzling grill. It was then that she saw a flash of blue from the corner of her eye. Her heart jumped, and slowly she turned to look out the window. . . and saw the old woman walking up the path.

She was wearing a coat that looked as if it had been cut from the sky.

❖ ❖ ❖

Arian had started to live in her body. It had happened yesterday, the moment she had placed her hand on her womb and felt the moon rising up to greet her. How could she possibly betray her body anymore when she had the moon running through her veins?

And the amazing thing about living in her body was that it required no thought, no planning. The only thing required was that she let her body be what it was. Her body had so much to tell her, so much to show her, if only she had listened to it all these years. But she was too busy trying to get her body to look like what everyone expected it to look like. She was too busy trying to get it to conform—to bend it into the perfect shape.

And it was never perfect enough. Her striving was endless. Real perfection was always one step away, until now, and now everything had changed. For she was no longer living alongside her body, she was living *in* it.

Never had the water been such a froth of crazy blue, never had the birds sung more beautifully, never had she felt the ecstasy—almost pain, it was so poignant a feeling—of rain on her face. She was so full, it felt as if every cell she was made of had grown to ten times its previous size.

She found that when she opened herself this wide, her emotions came swimming in. She felt fear manifest itself in her knuckles as a creeping, kind of tickling sensation. As she let the fear stay there, as she stopped trying to deny its existence in her body, an amazing thing happened—the fear became disinterested and left all on its own, and in its place came joy.

Arian sensed the joy rolling back and forth on the soles of her feet. She breathed the joy in, inhaled it deep down into her body so she wouldn't lose it, so she wouldn't miss it, and it quickly spread to all of her organs and limbs, a yellow and orange glaze, beating through her body, a steady high heat.

And everything was like that. She didn't have to find anything to keep her occupied anymore. She could just sit and be content with not moving, for everywhere she looked, touched or listened, the world was coming alive under her fingertips.

It is your body, the moon had told her, *not your mother's body. Not your lover's body. It is your body. Use it. Live through it, not around it. It is time for you to own your body—it is time you claimed it.*

Her body told her things she had never known. It showed her things she had never seen. It stopped being her enemy. It stopped being something she hated. She became precious, she became lovely, she became whole—when she stopped defining herself as the sum of her parts.

And so she was given the second gift of the moon the gift of comprehension.

The moon began to explain to her why she had deserted her own body, why she hadn't seen or smelled or tasted until now.

She heard the whispers first. The whispers that she knew so well. Whispers that dismantled women's bodies and spoke the language of separation. *Did you see her ass, can you believe the size of those thighs?* The language of body parts—of tits, of ankles, of breasts. Language filled with cold, metallic adjectives like *big, fat, too much.*

This was a language that had done its job well, a language filled with heavy, non-porous words that Arian had used as bricks, so that by the time she was twenty eight years old, she had managed to construct a fortress, whose purpose was to keep her body separate from her soul.

Arian knew that she was not the only one who had built this wall. There were others who had built and others who passed on the knowledge of how to build. She had been born with the knowledge, it was in her blood—handed down to her, from generation to generation.

Their bodies had been taken away from them, made public property when they were very young. They were put on display and left exposed. The softest places, the hidden places—the places where their souls once lived. They were left exposed.

But it could have been different! Oh, how it could have been different. Imagine if she had been taught to fight. Imagine if she had been taught *not* to go along with the abduction of her body. Imagine if she had *not* picked up her head and listened whenever some one judged her by the thickness of her thighs, by the fertile or infertile ground of her womb, by the size of her breasts.

But nobody had ever told her. Nobody she knew had ever dared speak it. There was silence, though. Muffled laughter behind cupped hands. Finger-pointing and blessed relief at not being the one who was being pointed at this time around.

Arian was in River when all these thoughts, all these memories and realizations finally came together. She found herself crying for the second time that morning as River surrounded her.

River moved in to hold her, to comfort her, and Arian suddenly realized the truth about River. It came to her simply and clearly—she was floating in a giant collection of tears—the tears of women, all the women who had come before her.

Arian sobbed then. She sobbed for her great-grandmother, a woman with lips the color of dahlias and almond eyes. She cried for her grandmother and then for her mother, not knowing yet why she cried for these women, but knowing she must.

Arian screamed as she felt her body filling with the bones of her mother, of her grandmother, of her grandmother's mother. She felt their blood mixing with her own. She felt each one of them rising up in her, making themselves known.

Her grandmother pushed her way into Arian's chin, her mother ran into her hands, and the woman with the almond eyes laid down in her feet.

The three of them stepped out of the woods at the same time—in perfect unison—with identical steps and got their first glimpse of the girl who swallowed the moon.

She was naked, her body the color of bark. It wasn't her nakedness that shocked them, for it did not look out of place, not here, at the river. What shocked them was the liquid moon that had begun to collect itself on the edges of her body. There was a ring of gold around her face, at the very edges of her hairline. They could barely see it, but it was there. It had also collected around the corners of her mouth.

Her nipples were gold with silver flecks—a round, shining planet in the center of each of her small breasts. They watched her as she brought her hands up to her face, as she began screaming. Her fingernails were the color of the harvest moon.

Yes, the moon was coming out in her. Her pregnancy had begun to show. Her stomach was as flat as a board, but she was slowly turning gold.

At first the girl didn't notice them standing there. She appeared to be staring right at them but her eyes were unfocused, blurry with her tears. It hurt them to see her screaming so. Her screams made their way through them like beating fists. Mana heard Temu utter a small cry of sympathy, and then she moved to go to her.

"No!" Mana whispered, "Don't go."

"But she's hurting so much! I've got to help her. I can't just stand here and do nothing!" said Temu.

"Yes, you can," said Urd, "and you must."

Temu stayed where she was, but her hands traveled up to her face, echoing the girl's movements. Soon she began sobbing silently with the girl who swallowed the moon. Before long, all three of them were crying with her. They couldn't help it. Her pain was so evident, so real.

After awhile, the girl noticed Urd standing there on the banks of River.

When Urd saw her eyes focus upon her face, when she heard the girl gasp, she reached over and took Temu's hand.

"Now," she said. "Now, we can go." Together they stepped out from under the trees and walked down to the water's edge. Urd unbuttoned her shirt as she went. And when they reached the water she took the shirt off, a wrinkled pile of linen in her hand.

The old woman squatted down in the warm, shallow river and held the shirt up to the light. Then she dipped it in and began to scrub. Temu stood on the bank and watched her, wondering what she was doing. Urd turned around as she washed. "Sit, sit!" she whispered. Temu sank down to the ground, her legs tucked beneath her.

The eyes of the girl who swallowed the moon misted up again as she watched the old woman wash her shirt. The simple scrubbing of knuckles against cloth began the story. Began the story of the women in her.

Arian stepped into the dark. She stepped into the place from which Temu, Mana and Urd had just come. The first thing she did was to resurrect the woman with the almond eyes—the woman who had finally, after all these years, made her way into her great-granddaughter's feet.

There she was on the other side of the river, washing her clothes in the warm, black water. The water that carried every women's secrets on its back.

2

GREAT GRANDMOTHER

She had come down to the river with a basket of clothes. It was the only way she could escape his hardened eyes. The river was safe. It was a women's place. The woven basket of laundry served her purpose well.

A little girl walked behind her. She had liquid black eyes, long eyelashes and braids. She was wearing a red and green dress. She was a familiar-looking child. Your heart would have recognized her. You would have seen yourself in her moon-shaped face.

The woman looked out into the black waters of the river that she had known and loved since she was a girl. She looked and looked, as if she were searching for something she knew she would never find. As she gazed out upon the river, she slowly began to unbutton her shirt, then slipped it off her wrists.

She wore nothing underneath. It was mid-summer, but still her flesh rose. Her breasts were large and full, her back muscled. She let the shirt drop to one hand; then she picked up the bottom of her skirt and tucked it up into her belt.

She waded into the water and squatted. She held the shirt up to the sun, an offering, a gift to the sky, and then she bent her head down and began to scrub.

She scrubbed the shirt for an hour. She scrubbed it with her fists. She scrubbed until her knuckles bled and the shirt turned from white to pink. Finally, she stood up and wrung the water out of the cloth. Then she turned and walked up the bank to where her daughter sat. Her naked breasts swayed from side to side as she walked.

The little girl stared at her mother's breasts. They were overwhelming to her. She had never seen those breasts unclothed. She had lain against them, buried her head in them, but she had never seen them bared. And now, out here in the open, her mother's breasts were frightening.

Her mother took her chin in her hand and tilted her face up to sun. "I need you to do something."

The little girl nodded. She couldn't speak. Her mother's breasts rose above her, brown and golden, looking like something just-spilled. Her mother was crying. Her tears fell onto her daughter's face.

"Go now, take the laundry into the river." She pointed to the basket that lay on the sandy shore.

"You don't need to wash it. Just let the basket go."

The little girl spoke.

"But, Mother, if I do that, we will lose all our clothes." She looked longingly at the basket which she could see held her best dress.

Her mother squatted down then, so that they were at eye level. Immediately, the little girl began to cry. Something was terribly wrong—she knew that—but she didn't know what and she didn't know what to do about it. All she knew was that she was no longer safe.

Her mother kissed the tears from her daughter's eyes and pushed the hair back from her forehead. "We won't be needing those clothes anymore, darling. So we may as well get rid of them. All right?" She tipped her daughter's face up again and kissed her on the lips.

Her mother's face was warm and wet, and the two of them stayed like that for a moment, lips pressed together. To the little girl, it felt as if her mother was breathing life into her. Finally, her mother stood up. She picked up the shirt she had washed and shook it out. She put it on. It was soaking wet, and her nipples showed through the pink-streaked material. Her mother hugged her breasts and backed away from her daughter.

"Go on, now, be a good girl and get the basket. I'll be standing right here." The little girl had the same almond eyes as her mother. She even had the same flowery lips. She did as she was told. She went to the basket and picked it up. It was surprisingly heavy, but she was a strong five-year-old, used to carrying buckets of water.

Her prettiest dress, her Sunday dress, was on the top of the pile. It was pale blue with lavender ribbons. She looked back at her mother for reassurance as she waded into the water. Her mother stood watching her as she said she would. But all she could see was her mother's eyes, her face was covered by her hands.

The little girl walked on with her load. She stopped when the water came up to her shoulders. The river was warm and dark. She emptied her bladder into the waiting water. She turned around again, to see if her mother could tell what she had done, but her mother wasn't watching anymore. She was facing the trees.

The little girl reached out and touched the ribbons on her dress one last time. They were satiny smooth and put her at ease. "Good-bye, my dress," she whispered, knowing that she would never have another dress as beautiful. And with one last look, she pushed the basket from her and watched as it floated down river.

"Look, Mother!" she yelled. "The basket, it's floating!" It looked like a tiny boat to the girl, or maybe a very large bird's nest. But a few minutes later, it quietly sank.

It might have had something to do with the rocks with which her mother had lined the bottom of the basket, or it might have had to do with the water-logging of the wood. But the little girl set the basket free. And down into the black waters it sank like a stone.

Once it was covered by water, the stacked piles of clothing lifted and separated. One by one, the little girl dresses sank down into the darkness. When the last of the dresses had gone its own way, there lay uncovered a baby with almond eyes. And after a time, she, too, went down, following her sister's clothes to the bottom of the river, her tiny fingers reaching, reaching, after the pale blue dress with the lavender ribbons.

3

It was Mana who finally stopped it. She couldn't stand to see any more pain. She pushed her way out of the underbrush and ran down to the water. She gathered Arian up into her arms and went striding across River.

Temu and Urd watched from the other side of the bank, not moving to follow her until Mana had disappeared inside House. There was a canoe on the shore which they climbed into then, and Temu paddled them across.

Urd dipped her hands in River and said a silent hello. River, steeped in sadness, moved her wide eyes against Urd's hand, but did nothing else.

It was a solemn time. None of them had expected it to be—they thought that when they arrived at the river they would find rest, respite from their own hard journeys. Instead, they were greeted with the pain of Arian's journey, a pain so immense they nearly forgot their own.

Temu jumped out of the boat and pulled it up on the shore. She held a hand out to the old woman, who took it gratefully.

"Don't worry," Urd said, "you'll be fine after a good rest."

Temu nodded, unable to speak. She followed Urd up the path, past the carefully tended herb garden to the screen door—where they got their first waft of House's blueberry pancakes.

It was a wonderful smell. It told them that someone had been expecting them, waiting for them, and that they were safe. Temu began to cry with exhaustion and relief. Urd began to cry too, but she was crying for a different reason. She, too, was exhausted, but she was used to feeling that way. She was old, after all, and was almost always tired to some degree. Exhaustion wasn't enough to make her cry anymore. But House's blueberry pancakes were enough, for even though she had been away for a hundred years, those round, buttered miracles still had the unmistakable smell of love.

When Mana burst through the door with a dripping, unconscious Arian in her arms, House nearly jumped out of her chair. Mana was, without a doubt, the biggest woman she had ever seen. She had a presence about her, as if there were animals, plants and flowers living right under her shining, dark skin. House stood for a second, staring. Mana stared back.

"Is there a place where I can put her?" Mana whispered, finally, when she realized House was a bit too overwhelmed to talk.

"Of course, of course. . ." said House, wiping her hands on her apron. "You can put her right there on the porch bed."

Mana stepped around House and tenderly laid Arian down on the bed. She pulled the covers up over her and smoothed the hair from her forehead. She began to sing.

"Amazing," she said, when she had finished her song. "I never imagined she would look this way." Then she looked up at House. "Don't worry, she just fainted, that's all. She'll be fine in a couple of hours. It's best that she sleep it off."

She sounded so sure of herself, of her motherly instincts, that House just nodded. This woman left her speechless. She was wearing black army boots.

The screen door opened, and House heard two more pairs of feet walk in.

"Mmmmm, smells good!" she heard a familiar voice say. "Is that smell what I think it is?"

House shuffled around the corner. It couldn't be, oh, no, it couldn't be. Why, that voice sounded just like. . .

House started to tremble. She peered around the corner slowly, looking down at the floor. The old woman seemed to anticipate that she would do this, and she lifted up her skirts so House could see the peach brocade slippers. She even went so far as to stick out a foot and point it daintily. Then she let the skirts drop and she curtseyed.

"Oh, House, dear House. You can look up now. You know who I am," the old woman said.

"Lena?" whispered House softly, her gaze moving up the old woman's body. "Is that you, Lena?" Finally she looked into the old woman's eyes. She walked up close and looked deep into her eyes, and saw Lena smiling back at her.

"It's you, it's you, you've come back!" House began to laugh and cry at the same time. "You've come back, my sweet, sweet Lena." House danced around the kitchen; she waved her arms and spun Urd around in a circle.

Finally she stopped and just stood there, holding Urd's hands tightly in her own. The old woman finally spoke, then.

"It's Urd this time around," she said softly, a hand on House's wet cheek.

"Oh," breathed House and backed away. "I'm sorry."

"Nothing to be sorry about. But do take a look. What do you think?" asked Urd, holding her arms away from her body.

House stared. This old woman was very small—petite, you would probably call her—whereas Lena had been a tall woman, built much like herself. Urd had sharp blue eyes; she was all angles and straight edges. Lena had been solid and muscular, big hipped with long gray hair. Their bodies were completely different, but the eyes—deep down in those blue eyes—was her dear, old Lena. There was no mistaking that.

The two women stood smiling at each other. "You haven't changed a bit," said Urd, her eyes sweeping the room.

"I never change. I'm always the same House."

Urd heard a small cough. She reached behind her. "And this is Temu," she said, pulling the girl out in front of her. Temu was a tangle of curly red hair and long legs. She stuck out her hand and pumped House's arm back and forth.

"Well, hello," said House. "Aren't you full of energy?"

"Not really," she told House earnestly. "There's nothing I'd like better then to sink into one of those nice big beds I see you have in there." Temu craned her head curiously, looking into the bedroom with pale green walls.

House turned and looked with her. "Well, that just happens to be your room, Temu. You're welcome to go in there and do whatever you want. Fall asleep, read a book. Whatever."

"Can I eat some of those pancakes?" asked Temu, looking over at the steaming platter that House had just placed on the kitchen table.

"Why, of course, I made them just for you," said House, winking at Urd. Temu ran over to the table.

Mana walked out of the porch bedroom and palmed the top of Temu's head affectionately. Temu was eating furiously and looked up with a full mouth and smiled. House extended her hand to the big woman. "I'm afraid we haven't been properly introduced," she said. "I'm House."

"Oh, nonsense," said Mana and pulled House into her arms. "I felt as if I had known you all my life as soon as I walked in that door."

House let herself be hugged. As Mana held her, she felt what she had seen under Mana's skin in that first glance. Mana was all encompassing, a walking planet. She was completely self contained. There was a tiny part of every living thing inside her.

"Your gardens are very beautiful," Mana said, stepping back.

"Oh," said House. "Can you see them from here?"

"No, I don't need to see them. I can smell them. The scent of things that grow pervades everything."

"All I can smell are those pancakes," said Urd. "How about it, shall we join Temu?"

The four of them sat at the table. Within minutes, Temu and Mana felt their rememberings lifting from them, as if House's pancakes relieved them of the burden, lifted the pain and terror right off them.The rememberings were still there, but they had moved to a more distant place so Mana and Temu could relax, replenish and refuel. The rememberings would come back when it was time, but for now, there were pancakes and fresh clean beds waiting for them.

There was a home that could fit them all.

4

GRANDMOTHER

Arian continued to remember. She was conscious of the huge, dark-skinned woman who picked her up and carried her to bed, pulled the covers up around her naked, wet body and sang her a lullaby of flowers and sun. But still, her remembering went right on.

Arian sat up in bed and looked out across the river, just in time to see a woman stepping out of the woods. She was quiet and small and walked with the sensitivity of someone who knew she was going where she belonged.

She came out of the blueberry bushes, one hand pushing them aside, the other holding her stomach protectively. She was pregnant, beautifully so. Her cheeks were pink and flushed, her skin clear and glowing.

She sighed as she came in full view of the river. It was a special place for her, a place of sacredness and beauty. She stood with her hands tucked beneath the curve of her abdomen and took the river up into her bones. After a while, she moved down the bank to the water.

She was barefoot, and she waded in up to her ankles. Her ankles were swollen, but strong. She balanced the extra weight of her baby well. Every once in a while she would reach up and run her palms in tiny circles over her belly and she would chant.

"Please, please, please," she said.

Her eyes became heavy as she moved into deep thought. She came to know, as she chanted, that her words could no longer keep her from the horror of the truth.

She was turning into her mother.

The more she became convinced of that, the more she continued to beg and to pray to be saved—for someone to save her from what she knew was inevitable.

Arian knew immediately who this woman was. There was no mistaking it. She was the very image of her mother. And because she was her mother's daughter, she, too, had came down to the river, knowing that no matter what, the river understood. The river provided peace and never laid blame. The river just went on.

The daughter had grown up in the fifteen years since she had let go of that laundry basket, and she was about to give birth to a child of her own. She had always looked forward to that day, thinking that having a child would be the final separation, the final wall that would stand tall enough to keep her and her mother separated for good. She thought that having children would allow her to stop being a child herself, allow her to stop reliving that day when she had killed her baby sister. She had thought it would stop the memories that haunted her—the pale blue dress, the lavender ribbons, the tiny, dimpled hand buried beneath all of her best clothes.

But the closer she got to giving birth, the closer she seemed to feel to her mother. It was frightening, her pregnancy became a path that led straight back to what she had been trying to escape, and now that she was on the verge of motherhood, something in her was opening. A door that had been shut for a long, long time. A door that led into a room where previously there had been only darkness.

It was an unentered place, dusty with disuse. Nobody had opened this door in many years. But now that a child grew in her belly, that door had opened just a crack, and through the crack the morning light flooded in. The window to the room was wide open, and the air of her impending motherhood was cleaning that room right out.

It was an ancient room, filled with abandoned, outgrown child's treasures—a rust-red cart, dolls with yarn hair, a blue ball. It was the room in which her mother lived, the room in which all banished mothers lived. All of the bad mothers, all of the failed mothers, all of them sent there by their daughters.

This was the room that contained her mother's laugh, that held her mother's tears, the shaking of her back, the jamming of her mother's fist into her mouth so that she wouldn't be heard screaming as her baby went into the river.

Yes, this was the room that held her mother's screams, that pinned those screams into her body, that pummeled them there, that beat them into those beautiful breasts. And this was the mother that her daughter had never seen—the mother who spent day after day sitting in the doorway on a hard wooden chair, staring out into the dusty darkness, trying to remember the sound of her daughter's laugh.

The pregnant woman walked up to the door of this room. She was beautiful, full with life. She had everything she could possibly want. Her mother sat on the other side of the doorway, waiting silently for her daughter to let her out. She sat waiting as she had been waiting for years.

She heard the sound of her daughter's hand on the doorknob, and her hopes rose like a great, gleaming whale. The light streaming in from the crack in the door felt so good. Did she dare hope, did she dare to think the time had come?

The door opened a little, and the pregnant woman looked in. The first thing she saw was her mother's feet. Her mother was barefoot, sitting in this room. In fact, she was naked, but the daughter never found this out. She took one look at those feet and slammed the door so fast the dust went flying. She couldn't stand it. Those feet were exactly the same as her own.

The old woman sat without moving as the darkness settled into the room once more. There was still the faint smell of light around her, and she held onto it as long as she could. When the darkness had risen and moved over her head she began to scream again, silently, her hands curled up into fists that were crammed into her open mouth.

The pregnant woman left the river then. She walked out of the warm, soothing waters, back up the hill and disappeared into the woods. Her back was straight, her heart was hard.

And the room in which her mother sat was dark.

"Well, that was the best meal I've had in a hundred years," said Urd, winking at House. She folded up her napkin and put it on the table.

Temu yawned in agreement. She had eaten eight of House's pancakes herself.

"Time for bed," said Mana, pushing herself back from the table. "House, we'll help do the dishes when we get up," she said, tucking her chair in neatly.

House nodded and finished a bite of pancake.

"Don't worry about that, just go and sleep. First bedroom on your right." She pointed with her fork. "It's all ready for you."

After Temu and Mana left, House began stacking the plates on the table. Urd moved to help her.

House looked at her in surprise. "Well, what's gotten into you?" she asked.

"Can't somebody change their bad habits?" asked Urd laughing. "It may have taken me a hundred years, but I've learned," she said proudly.

"Well, it's about time," snorted House.

They cleaned up silently for a while. They didn't need any words, they just needed to move around the kitchen as they had done so many years ago in the same, familiar patterns—House stacking plates and bringing them to the sink, Urd wrapping the leftover food and putting it in the icebox, each moving knowingly around the other's body in the small kitchen.

There was the sound of the sink filling up, the after-meal ritual of House picking her teeth with a toothpick, staring out the window into the trees and water. It was all the same. None of it had changed.

"I can't believe you're back," said House finally, her back to Urd. Her voice was swollen, plump with emotion.

"I can't believe it either. But I'll tell you, there's no place I'd rather be in the entire world than with you, here. I didn't know until I walked in that door how much I missed you. How much of myself I left here, how much of myself is still buried in these walls of yours, House. I didn't know."

House turned around and held out her arms to Urd.

"Come here," she said. The old woman walked quickly into her arms. House held the small body to her large one. It was a strange body to her—a new body, not at all like Lena's had been. But she could feel Lena beneath this new shell. There was no mistaking that it was her. A different smell, a different shape, but it was Lena.

The two of them turned and looked out the kitchen window. It was another familiar posture, the memory of it giving them goose bumps.

"Well, what do you think?" asked Urd.

"What do I think about what?" said House, picking her teeth again and staring absentmindedly into the trees.

"About this crew I brought with me?"

House turned and looked at Urd. "About your crew?" House tossed her head back and roared. "I think we are in for it, that's what I think! I just hope we aren't in over our heads. But I figure you wouldn't have come back here if it wasn't for something really important."

Urd sighed. "Yes, you're right House, as usual. It is important. Wait until you find out who those two are!"

"Well, who are they?" House asked.

"I can't say. They must be the ones to tell you that. They are a lot of work, though, that I can tell you. But you must have had your hands full too, with *her*." Urd cocked her head back to the porch where Arian was sleeping.

House nodded solemnly. "That's an understatement. But she's a brave, intelligent, capable girl. And she has the knowing buried deep down in her bones. No mistaking that, it's just a question of uncovering it, of bringing it to the surface. She impresses me, that one."

House added in a tender voice, "and I think I am growing to love her. I keep thinking about how I will miss her when she's gone. Something tells me she will be gone soon, that our time together is short. And it's shorter still, now that you all have arrived. Isn't that right?" she asked Urd.

"Yes," sighed Urd. "Our time is almost up. But what worries me is that there is still so much to do. I don't know if. . ." The old woman yawned.

"Where are my manners!" said House. "You must be exhausted! Shall I show you to your bedroom? Not that you need to be shown," she added.

"Yes, I think that's probably a good idea. We'll have plenty of time to catch up. Besides, I won't be of much help if I don't get some rest today, too. I've got to pay attention to this old body."

The two of them linked arms and walked down the hallway. "Let the three of us sleep until it's time to make dinner." Urd instructed House." Then wake us up. Tonight, we will have our first meal together, all of us, including Arian. After dinner, we'll talk. May as well get right down to business. She's not really sleeping, you know. She's still going through her rememberings' and if my calculations are correct, she'll be finishing up just about dinnertime."

They arrived at Urd's bedroom, and House opened the door. Urd walked in and her hands fluttered up to her face.

"Oh, House, it's still here. It's exactly the same!" Urd walked around the room in a slow circle. She picked up a robin's egg from the bookcase, she ran her hands over the quilt, she stood by the open window and breathed deeply. "It even smells the same." She turned to House and smiled.

"You haven't changed a thing have you, you sentimental old thing," she said to House, her voice low and teasing. "Why, it's as if this room has been waiting for me all these years. It's as if it knew I was coming back!"

"I think it did. I think I did, too." The tears sprang to House's eyes again as she looked at her best friend standing by the window. "And the window. . ." House sniffled. "I've even left the window open all these years!"

"Well, my dear one, you've done well," said Urd as she walked over to House. She handed her a handkerchief that had been buried deep in her pocket. "Here, wipe your nose. I'm back now, so there's no need to cry." But the old woman had tears in her eyes, too.

House finally left, but it was a long time before Urd got to sleep. She lay for hours in that old, familiar bed, remembering the cracks in the ceiling, the basket of round black river stones, the paintbrushes encrusted with old color. Finally, she fell asleep and when House came to check on her later, she found the old woman covered up to her neck in blankets, her head turned toward the open window so that she would not miss the sun on her face.

5

MOTHER

The next woman to step out of the woods was someone Arian knew immediately. It was her mother. And like the two women who had come before her, she was quite beautiful. She had the same almond eyes and straight white teeth.

She picked her way through the blueberry bushes daintily. She was dressed in pedal pushers and a sleeveless shirt. Her eyes were clear and shiny. Her hair was short, brown swirls all over her head.

She sat down on a rock and took off her sneakers. Her shirt and pants came off next and she stood there for a moment in her white bra and panties. Her body was tender and still growing. She was breathtaking in the simplicity of her cotton underwear. She was brave, she was unafraid. She ran to the river and dove in.

She was a pleasure to watch in the water. Her limbs were strong and worked well. Someone had taught her how to swim.

Recently her father had forbid her to go to the river. "You're too old for that," he said. "No more swimming out in the open where everyone can see you."

"But Dad," she had said. "There's never anyone there but me."

"I don't care!" he had roared. "I forbid you to go."

But her mother knew what the river meant to her daughter and when her husband's back was turned she said, "Go, quickly, I'll tell him you are at the store." And so she had taken off, running fast down the path through the woods that led to her beloved river.

As she turned somersaults in the water she thought of her mother's sweet complicity. How the two of their heads had touched, forehead to forehead as they bent together and whispered. It made her feel warm, as if the two of them were best friends. It made her feel taken care of, protected, keeping this small secret from her father.

She was smiling as she thought of her mother. Floating on her back, her breasts in her bra were two white peaks rising up from the river. She traced circles with a wet finger on her flat stomach. The sun and river on her nearly naked body felt so good. The river held her gently and lovingly. The river held her as she imagined the husband she would have one day would hold her.

What could possibly be wrong with that?

What was wrong was the intent of the dark eyes that watched her from the edge of the woods—staring at those young breasts that rose so temptingly out of the water, staring at those cotton panties that showed the dark triangle between her legs so well when she scissor-kicked.

He waited until she was done with her swim, until she emerged from the river, the water falling from her limbs. He waited until she turned around, until he saw her shoulder blades. He waited until then to grab her and throw her on the banks of the river, tearing off the bra and tying it savagely around her mouth so she couldn't scream. He ripped her panties away and looked up at the sky then, to avoid seeing her eyes as he pounded himself into her, as his hands pumped her breasts, the ground scraping the skin off her back and buttocks until they were raw and bleeding.

Within minutes he was done. He ran off into the woods, his workboots leaving large, dark prints in the muddy banks.

The young woman lay not moving, her eyes unfocused, looking straight up. Like the man who had just raped her, she, too, had stared at the sky. She would think of that later—that the both of them had the same bit of blue imprinted on their brains. Blueness that shattered with the pain of the two stares. Blue sky that rained down on the two of them, that had fallen deep into the river and lay pulsing and glinting in the silt and soft sand.

After a while she sat up, moaning with pain. There was blood all over her, perfect crimson prints of his large hands on her breasts. But most of it was between her legs.

She was in shock but managed somehow to get up and put her clothes on. She used her panties and bra to wipe away the blood and sperm, then she buried them in a hole in the soft mud of the river bank.

She was naked as she bent over on her hands and knees, digging with her bare hands in the mud. Her pale body was a shocking white against the deep brown of the river soil. She no longer felt the pleasure of the sun on her back, she no longer held her body like it was young and beautiful. And she kept her eyes on the ground.

She didn't know how she made it home. The thought of her mother kept her going. Her mother would know what to do. Her mother would help her.

She staggered in the back door praying that her father was downstairs in the workshop. "Ma, Ma. . ." she moaned. She heard the shuffle of her mother's slippers on the linoleum floor. "What is it?" she heard her say. "What's wrong?"

The mother saw her daughter leaning against the door frame, one hand between her legs to stop the flow of blood, the other arm covering her full breasts, which were clearly visible beneath the wet blue cotton of her sleeveless shirt.

Her mother gasped and put her hands to her mouth. At first her eyes were soft, compassionate, filled with tears, but almost immediately they hardened, as she saw her daughter's breasts so clearly revealed.

Her mother stood staring at her. She had never seen her daughter's breasts before. They were large, full breasts and they swayed as her daughter staggered toward her, her hands extended for help.

The mother felt a sour taste rising in her mouth. She didn't know where it came from—she didn't know what it was about; all she knew was that her daughter had breasts that swayed just like some other woman that she had known long ago .

She took her hand down from her mouth and said coldly, "Well, what do you expect, swimming in your underwear? You were probably asking for it." She sighed heavily, crossing her arms in front of her, looking her daughter up and down. She looked more harshly at her daughter than the stranger who had watched her from the woods. She judged, she cast sentence and she turned her back.

She turned her back on her daughter and reached under the sink. Her rough hands searched for the container of rags so that she could wipe the hand prints of blood from her daughter's breasts.

Deep within the purple shame of her mother's withering glance, the daughter did what she had to to survive. It was an initiation day for her, a rite of passage, for this was the day in her young life that she, too, shut the door to a little room in her heart.

And left her mother there, sitting alone in the dark.

PART SIX

GOING ABOUT THEIR WORK

1

It was turning out to be a beautiful day. House finished cleaning up and put some hot water on to boil. She walked quietly into the porch bedroom, stealing a quick look at Arian who still seemed to be asleep. She kneeled down and opened the dresser drawer.

The drawer was almost empty. House didn't have too many clothes—a few work dresses, three aprons and one warm sweater. It was really all she needed. She never went further then the gardens, after all.

House moved aside the neatly folded stacks of aprons and dresses and reached behind them. She was searching for something special. Something not every day. Her hands touched the well- worn cotton and she brought the dress out, smiling when the yellow-green cloth came into view. It was her acorn dress, exactly the color of those sweet nuts that sat so beautifully in their brown bark dishes.

She held it up to her face and inhaled. It smelled of the pine dresser and faintly of lemon. She stripped, peeling her clothes off in one smooth gesture. Then she slipped the dress on over her head and it fell in a fragrant heap down to her ankles. It was a loose, flowing dress, a dress that fit her large limbs well. She felt graceful, almost beautiful in this piece of wonderful cloth.

House walked back into the kitchen, her hairbrush in one hand. While she waited for the kettle to whistle, she took her hair down from its usual bun and let it fall to her waist. Her hair was a surprise. Nobody knew it was so long or so beautiful. House sat down and began to brush her hair. She tipped her head back and sighed as she brushed. So rare a thing it was, for her to have time to do this. It was a luxury that she delighted in.

She got up from the chair when the kettle began to whistle and poured herself a cup of tea. It was quiet inside, mid-morning, and everyone was asleep in their bedrooms. House listened for a second, to the stillness, then she took her tea and walked outside.

She leaned over the porch railing as River swam up.

"Isn't it wonderful?" she whispered. "Lena's come back."

"Ah, yes it is," said River. "And she hasn't changed a bit."

"You don't think so? But she looks completely different!"

"No, she doesn't, House. Just look right past her body. I knew it was her when I saw her on the shore. I didn't even have to look in her eyes."

"Oh, River it's always that way with you," said House, waving her hand in the air. "You believe so easily. I wish I could do that. I would have figured out it was her coming a long time ago if that was the case. But I had to wait until she was staring me in the face. Until I heard her voice."

"You just need to trust yourself more," said River, sinking deep into the couch of her waters. House nodded and took a sip of her tea.

"Oh, I'm sad, House, so sad," said River, her water moving slowly from side to side.

"I'm sad because of the rememberings. Arian's remembering now, and it's all buried down deep in my waters. There are so many women's stories, and always they have made their way down to the river. Instinctively they have known that I am a place that heals. Now it is Arian's turn to stand on that bank — to make her way out of the woods. I just hope she can get through this—that she has the strength to move through. "

House glanced at the porch bedroom.

"She's not sleeping, then?" she asked.

"No," answered River. "She's remembering. I just showed her her mother. That was probably the worst. The other women, her grandmother and her great-grandmother are far enough removed for her to keep some distance, but there's no turning away from her mother's pain.

Now she has a choice to make. Will she continue the legacy that has been passed on from great-grandmother, to grandmother to mother? Will she become another generation, another daughter in a chain of mothers and daughters who have been denying each other since the beginning of time? Will she participate in the legacy of blame? Or will she pick her head up—will she refuse to continue looking at the ground? Will she hear, will she truly hear the stories and be able to reach one long arm back into the past and unlock that door?"

"Oh, River, why does there have to be such pain?" whispered House, leaning over, her hair dipping into the water.

"It's important pain, House. It's necessary. Don't you see that?"

House shook her head.

River swam up to the dock and lifted herself up over the side. "We need the pain, House," she said gently.

"Without the pain, without moving through the darkness, there would be no going forward. That's what Arian is doing. That's what all these women have been doing. Nothing can stop them. Nothing can prevent it from happening. They must be willing to stay put when the darkness falls."

"Urd, Urd, it's time to wake up." House knocked gently at the door.

"Come in, House," Urd murmured.

House opened the door slowly. "Are you awake yet? Should I come back?"

"Oh, no," said the old woman. "I've been waiting for you. Here, come sit a bit," she patted the quilt beside her.

House walked over, a smile on her face. "It's strange, yet so familiar to see you in that bed," she said. "It's as if you never left. You're in the same position you used to sleep in, your head turned towards the window. The only difference is that your feet used to stick off the end of the bed, your legs were so long." House lifted up the covers and looked underneath. "Looks like you don't have that problem anymore!" she teased softly.

"Stop that, you old pest," said Urd affectionately. "And don't be making fun of the fact that I came back short. Now, help me get out of bed. And what should I wear for dinner? I am going to finally meet her, aren't I? Do you have anything that would fit me?" she asked House, staring down at her scrawny ankles.

Urd turned her feet from left to right. "Probably not, but all I brought was that one dress and it's filthy from the journey. It's hardly appropriate for a first meeting. What do you think?"

House was ruffling through Lena's old clothes in the closet. "How about these?" she asked, holding up a pair of jeans that were neatly pressed on a hanger. "Oh, I loved those jeans," said Urd. "Yes, let's try those. I can roll them up. And that shirt, the one with the flowers. That was my favorite shirt. I'll wear that, too."

House pulled the clothes from the closet and helped Urd to roll up the legs and sleeves so they fit. "They smell like you, House," said Urd, putting her hair up into a bun with one smooth gesture.

"There, now." She turned around and presented herself to House. "How do I look?"

House laughed. "You look fine—I don't think you have to worry. She's the one who will be nervous."

"Nonsense," said Urd. "There's nothing to be nervous about. She's out in the kitchen?"

House nodded.

"Have you told her about us?"

"Yes."

"Did you tell her I was Lena?"

"I did; she took it rather well, I thought. She didn't seem surprised."

"Good, that's good. Out of my way," Urd stood up and pushed House gently to the side.

House followed the old woman into the kitchen. She watched, as Urd pushed away the arm Arian extended in greeting and hugged her instead. The girl towered above Urd, who looked dwarfed in her arms. Finally, Urd backed away and took a good look at Arian.

"Well, you certainly did swallow the moon, didn't you?" she pronounced and turned Arian's face from left to right in the light. She pulled the girl's hair back and investigated the faint ring of gold that was manifesting itself in a perfect circle around her hairline and jaw.

"Amazing," said Urd solemnly. "I've never seen the moon like this before." Abruptly she let Arian's face go. Arian rubbed her jaw where Urd had held it a little too tightly.

"Are you afraid of me?" Urd asked.

Arian moved closer. "I'm not sure," she answered, "let me check."

She bent down and took the old woman's face in her hand and moved it from left to right in the light, exactly as Urd had just done to her. Urd allowed this, although she had a look of surprise in her blue eyes. Still, she let the girl peer into her face.

Urd felt the light of the moon coming out of Arian's eyes. It was a soft, subtle light, and it moved right into her heart. Arian looked deep into Urd and lit up her insides with the moon. It was a jeweled sensation, as if Arian had filled her chest cavity with sprinklings of tiny diamonds.

"Is this what it feels like to you?" Urd gasped, her eyes shut tight with the sensation.

"Yes," answered Arian. "Only more so." She gave Urd a shower of sapphires and then let her go. Urd felt the jewels melting silently and softly inside her and she sighed.

"Well," said Urd, when the feeling was all gone, "that was quite remarkable." She held her hand over her heart. "And did you find what you were looking for?"

"Yes," said Arian. "It's as I thought. I know who you are."

Urd nodded approvingly. She smiled and put her hand up to Arian's cheek. "How nice that you still recognize me." That tender moment lasted but a second, and then Urd was all business.

"Now, have you met the other two yet?"

"No, they're still sleeping, I think."

"Not for long," said Urd, and she walked off down the hallway to get them up.

Arian shrugged her shoulders at House and then went back to the cutting board.

"Well, what do you think?" whispered House coming up behind her and grabbing a piece of red pepper .

"Meeting her is like somebody just handed a piece of myself back to me. She is a part of me that lives somewhere in the future. Does that make sense? She is a stranger but a relative all at the same time," said Arian.

"Mmmm," House murmured while taking tiny bites out of the pepper. Urd walked into the room with Mana and Temu on her arms.

"Arian, dear, come here. I would like you to meet Mana and Temu."

Mana stepped forward first. "Hello," said Mana warmly. "It's so nice to finally meet you—under normal circumstances, I mean." Arian wiped her hands on her pants and then took Mana's hands in her own.

"Thank you for carrying me out of River," she said softly. "I remember that. And I remember your song. I hope I will be fortunate enough to hear your voice again."

"Oh, you'll hear her sing again," said a small voice behind Mana. "She sings to me all the time."

Temu crept out from her hiding place behind Mana and ran up

and kissed Arian's cheek. "I've been so looking forward to meeting you!" She grinned shyly at Arian, "I hope we are going to be friends."

"I hope so, too, Temu. I could use a friend." Arian reached out and picked up one of Temu's curls and held it in her hand. "What stunning hair you have," she said.

"You think my hair is pretty?"

"No, I think it is beautiful," said Arian. "And I have a feeling I'm not the only one who feels that way."

Temu blushed, and bent her head, thinking of the hands that had pulled her down through the earth.

"Well!" said Urd, clapping her hands together. "Now that we have done the introductions, shall we get on with the making of dinner?" She walked over to the screen door and stuck her face up against it, looking from left to right and then up to the sky. She sniffed deeply.

"It looks like it's going to be a beautiful night. It's entirely too nice to sit inside, suppose we set up the table in the garden?" Urd started barking out directions.

"Some things never change," House whispered to Arian with an affectionate smile. "She was always bossy."

"House, are you listening to me? You're in charge of supervising dinner. You can have Temu as well as Arian at your disposal. Now, Mana, you need to get the table set up outside, and I know I don't have to tell you to be careful maneuvering it around those gardens. We don't want any of those plants and flowers crushed."

"And you, Urd?" asked House, because she was the only one who could get away with asking. "What will you be doing?"

"I will be thinking, of course," the old woman answered. "And planning. Now come here, House, before you start supper. I have an idea I want you to help me with." The two of them walked out through the screen door, Urd whispering into House's ear.

2

Arian was amazed at what she could do now that the moon was growing in her. It was a strange pregnancy. Her belly was not becoming fat, for the moon did not seem to be growing *out* in her. It seemed to be growing *up*.

She felt it rising, centimeter by centimeter. The golden liquid just kept getting higher the longer the moon remained in her body. The higher up her body it rose—the more of the moon's consciousness she seemed to gain.

Arian really noticed it when the three women arrived. Until then, it had been just her, River and House, so she hadn't had much of a chance to note any changes. But when she met Temu, Mana and Urd, she realized that things were really happening.

She found herself able to see with the moon's eyes. She could see inside people. Being able to do this gave her a feeling of power. It was scary, but she also liked this strength. For the first time in her life, she felt that her body was her own. She was learning how to use it, how to live in it. That alone was making her strong, helping her find a center she had never known.

So far, she had control of this moon-given power. She seemed to be able to call it up and let it go at will, as she had when she looked at Temu. If she had wanted, she could have gone much deeper, could have sat herself right down in the girl's stomach, could have known exactly how those hands felt wrapped around her ankles, the sweet and sour taste of the pomegranate seeds he had placed on her tongue.

But something told her to shut it off. It would have been wrong to continue unless she had been invited. Arian knew, however, that it was only a matter of time before the moon rose in her again. Its ultimate destination was her mouth, and its birth passage would be her throat.

There would be no stopping its coming forth.

3

The kitchen was filled with laughter. House could hear it from out in the garden where she was stooped over, cutting big bunches of chives and dill for dinner. It made her smile. The memories went shooting through her, leaving her thirsty and yearning, aching with being so full.

It had been a long time since she had had so many people here. This evening was like old times. It was how she liked it best—the screen door screeching back and forth, voices moving through the air, calling, calling to one another in the night. Crickets in the background, a small breeze in the air. The rocky smell of the stars that were beginning to appear.

House hugged herself and listened. It was as if their voices were all that existed, all that was important in the world at this very moment.

House stood up, one hand on her back and wiped the sweat off her forehead. It was still hot, even though the sun had almost completely set. She could still see the last bits of the day, an orange-yellow glow, setting fire to the trunks of the oak trees.

House looked up into the lavender sky. You just didn't get those colors in the winter. Winter skies were bright red and crimson, but summer was pale blues and violets. And once in awhile, if you were really lucky, you got a lavender sky, like tonight.

The screen door opened, and House watched as Mana stepped out, the dining room table in her hands. She carried it effortlessly. House could smell onions and garlic frying as the door slowly closed behind her.

"Hello," said Mana as she walked by. She was humming some bit of a song that sounded very familiar, but it wasn't until she had drifted out of sight that House realized what she had been singing. She was singing the rain.

House looked at the two piles of fragrant herbs she had clutched in her hands. She brought them up to her nose and inhaled. It never failed to amaze her that such good things grew from the earth. She never took it for granted, her surprise and gratitude were always the same. Each time she bent to pick something for dinner, she gave thanks.

She stood up, wiping the wet knife on her apron.

"Mana, do you need any help down there?" she yelled.

"No, thanks, I'm all set."

House could still hear her humming. She watched for a minute as Mana got down on her hands and knees and gently moved some snapdragons out of the way so the legs of the table wouldn't crush them. The flowers seemed to move magically under her hands, or maybe it was just the darkening light.

House walked back inside. Temu and Arian were at the stove cooking, Temu emptying a plate of corn into a pot of boiling water and saying something to Arian. The two of them laughed heartily, throwing their heads back, tossing their long hair.

They were nearly the same height, but Arian was rounded, softer. Temu still had the sharpness of *girl* about her. Temu turned around, holding a piece of corn in her hand.

"House, doesn't this look good?" she asked, waving the corn, and then House saw the softness was there after all; it had started to appear around the corners of her mouth.

"It does. Now, do you two have everything under control?"

Arian nodded and opened the oven door to check the potatoes. They were simmering away, all golden and brown, just short of crusty.

"How's Mana doing out there?" asked Urd.

"Fine," said Mana, walking in the door. "It's all ready, whenever you are."

"Five minutes," said Arian, the joy rising in her voice.

"Is everyone as happy as I am?" she asked, walking into the middle of the room, wooden spoon in one hand. She spun around on her heel, turning to look at all of them. "I can't remember a time when I have been happier! And all we're doing is making dinner. I'm not sure I understand it. It just feels right, having all of us here, like we fit."

Arian looked down and swallowed.

"It's like, it's like. . ." she started. "I almost can't describe it. It sounds crazy, I know. I only met you all this afternoon, but I feel as if I have known you all my life. And that nothing, *nothing* more should be happening right now then all of us here, gathered in this kitchen, making dinner. That's all there is. That's what's filling me up. The simpleness of the porch light shining through the dark woods. The smell of food cooking, House walking in that door. That lavender sky, our knowledge that the stars will come out. Our sureness that day after day, night will continue falling. There is nothing more than this. In all my life I've never felt so connected, so perfectly right. I could want nothing more than these moments."

Arian began to cry, her eyes brimming over.

"You speak for us all, I think," said Urd. The old woman's eyes were shining and bright.

"Come now, wipe your eyes, I think we are ready to eat."

Mana had done magic.

When they walked outside, each of them carrying a pot full of food, they got their first glimpse of where they were eating dinner —and gasped.

Mana had set up the oak table under the willow tree, right in the middle of the round garden, and the table was almost completely covered with a carpet of flowers.

The mix of colors was rich, and even though it was dusk and the light was quickly fading, the reds, oranges and golds still bloomed vibrantly in the coming dark. The flowers seemed to be moving and shifting ever so slightly.

"They move for me," Mana told them without a trace of vanity in her voice. "And they would do that for you, too," she added, "if you knew how to ask."

Arian watched in amazement as pale pink and white honeysuckle, red hollyhocks and feathery autumn sweet wound themselves right up the legs of the tables. The plants seemed to be dancing as they twined around each other intimately, leaf touching stalk, pollen on velvet petals. The only spot that was not covered by flowers was a round circle in the middle of the table.

"That's where the food goes," Mana told them, leading the way down the hill. They followed her single file to the table, each balancing a steaming pot in her hands.

When they came close, they formed a circle around the table and leaned in to put the food down. Mana clapped her hands lightly then, and they found themselves surrounded by soft, sparkling lights. The entire willow tree was bathed in dots of flickering warmth.

"It's magic," said Temu.

"Fireflies," Mana told them.

Years later, when River thought of that night, she did not remember the tablecloth, the flowers, or the firefly strings of light. What she remembered were their hands—withered old hands, plump young ones, hands as big as platters, hands whose veins ran gold, hands of all those women, reaching across that table.

That dinner was a moment plucked out of time. The breeze blowing from upriver, those voices rising up in the air. The five sets of hands moving over and over again, riding the sea of flowers gently, slowly, like a fleet of boats.

"It's hot in here," said Urd, wiping her brow with a handkerchief. Dinner was finished, and everything was cleaned up and put away. They had all collapsed on couches and chairs and were fanning themselves with books. The screen door was open in hopes that an evening breeze might come in, but the air was still .

Urd sat up. "I'm going for a swim. Anybody want to come?"

Mana smiled, "Temu, Arian?"

"Yes, yes!" they both jumped off the couch.

"Well, then, it's a plan. House, you don't mind if we go, do you?" asked Urd.

"Go," House waved them away. "I've got some sewing to do that I've put off long enough. Perhaps it will be cool enough to fall asleep by the time you come back."

Temu and Arian ran out, pushing one another out of the way to be the first one in the water. Mana and Urd walked out after them. They heard a splash, a yell, and then another splash. Urd took Mana's arm in her own, and the two of them strolled down the path to the water, smiling in the darkness as they walked. They could see the heads of Temu and Arian bobbing up and down. River was swimming in circles around them.

"Come in, come in!" yelled Temu. "It's beautiful. River is so warm."

"We're coming," yelled Mana. "Just give us a second."

A few minutes later Urd and Mana slid into the water.

"Ahhhhh," said Urd, "I'd forgotten what this felt like. . . swimming in River, swimming through the night."

The old woman's eyes were bright, gleaming in the darkness, her wet hair plastered to her head, bits of scalp showing through.

"Can you feel this night; can you feel it thick and moist around your head, in your ears, wrapping around your neck?" asked Urd, waving her hand in the air.

"You imagine the night is separate from you, that you have nothing to do with it until you begin to swim in it. And the further into the night you swim, the more those lines that have kept you separate begin to blur. Things no longer need to be cut up into neat little sections like sky, earth, grass and sun. The further into the night you swim, the less you need those things to be distinct. The less you need them to be in their proper places. The sky no longer must be up, the earth no longer must be under your feet. You begin to release the world of your demands, of your expectations, of your need to be safe by knowing things are where they should be."

Mana smiled her understanding at Urd, and the two of them floated in a comfortable silence. "May I have a ride?" Urd asked her a few minutes later. Mana nodded. She rolled over on her stomach and the old woman jumped on her back, wrapping her arms around Mana's neck.

Mana swam over to where Temu, Arian and River were talking.

"Let's go to the raft," Urd told them. "I'm getting cold." Everyone nodded and swam quickly to the wooden platform.

"Ah. . . blankets," said Urd, once she had gotten up. On the corner of the raft was a neatly folded pile of blankets set on top of a basket, obviously House's doing. Arian distributed the blankets. She stood examining what other goodies House had left. The others quickly wrapped themselves up and sat down.

"There are candles," reported Arian. "Shall I light them?"

" I don't think that will be necessary," said Urd. "You are giving off quite enough light by yourself."

Arian looked down at her body and gave a small gasp. She *was* glowing, her body outlined in gold and silver.

"You're beautiful," said Temu. "Look at her, Mana!"

"I'm looking. I've never seen anything like it."

Arian lifted her arms and ran her fingers down her sides. Then she pushed her hair back from her face and heard everyone gasp again.

"What, what is it?" she asked.

When Arian had pushed her hair back, they saw the moon clearly on her face.The circle around her hair and jaw had become absolutely defined, and now the gold was starting to move into her features. Her lips were draped in it, and her eyes were yellow with silver flecks.

"Is it okay, am I okay?" Arian asked them, her eyes filling with tears. "You still want to be with me, don't you?" she asked, panic in her voice.

"Of course," said Urd. "We're simply remarking on the changes in you."

"Good," Arian looked at all of them. "So stop staring at me, please. It makes me self-conscious." She began to rummage in the basket.

"House, you are such a dear!" Arian yelled into the night. There were two bottles of wine, five red apples and a plate of oatmeal cookies, freshly baked. "Who's hungry?" asked Arian, looking up from the basket.

"Take it all out, you might as well," said Mana.

Arian dragged the basket into the middle of the raft. Mana pulled the cork out of one of the bottles of wine and tipped her head back, taking a long swallow. "Good," she pronounced, "Almost as good as mine."

"Hand it over," said Urd. Mana passed the bottle to her and the old woman took an even longer drink.

When they had finished both bottles of wine, eaten four of the apples and the entire plate of cookies without speaking, there developed a sense of waiting. Expectancy. Temu, Mana and Arian all knew Urd had not brought them swimming for no good reason —the blankets and food were a sure sign of that. Urd had planned this with House.

There had already been much laughter and playing this night, and they knew the time for work was close. Each of them was nervous and excited at the same time. They waited patiently for the old woman to speak.

"I've not seen a night such as this, in all of my lifetimes," Urd said, finally, "First, I want to tell you how proud I am of all of you. Each of you has gone deeper, further than you ever thought possible to bring yourselves here."

Urd shut her eyes and spoke softly.

"Nothing could have stopped you, you know. I can tell you that now, now that we are here. Temu, nothing could have stopped you from picking that flower; Mana, nothing could have kept you from your grief; and Arian, nothing could have stopped you from swallowing the moon."

"That was the first half of the journey—each of you had to go back and remember where you had come from. Remember who you had been. Now, with this knowledge, you are ready to walk into the future. But you can't do that alone. And that's why we are here. The second part of this journey we have to take together. You have begun by remembering as an individual, but you will not complete yourselves until you remember together. And to do that you must tell one another your stories."

There was a long silence, in which each woman willed someone else to rise first. Finally Mana got up. "I will tell," she said, the blanket falling to her feet. She rose to her full height of seven feet on that small raft in the middle of the river, and she began to speak.

4

After they had all left, and House could hear their laughter echoing down the long road of the night, she went into Urd's room and got down on her hands and knees to look under the bed. She pulled out a box that was covered in dust, wiped off the cobwebs and dirt, and sat back on her ankles for a moment, considering what she had in front of her.

Slowly, she took the cover off. Her eyes widened when she saw the pieces of fabric. She hadn't remembered they were so beautiful. She shuffled through them, doing a damage check. It was all intact — no moth holes, no mouse droppings. The fabric was exactly as she had left it.

House carried the box to the kitchen, where she took each piece of cloth and spread it wide on floor. Then she sat for a while, letting the different textures and variations of tone and color seep into her head.

She dreamed, then. She let herself move into her imagination, and she dreamed of the most magnificent dress she had ever made. It would be the color of the sun, yet beneath that it would glow with the pale lavender of summer dusk. It would have sleeves made from the fringe of lilies and a skirt that smelled of lilacs. The neckline would rise and fall like the mountains and the hem would move like the wind.

It couldn't be anything less than this beautiful. House picked up her scissors and got down on the floor. Very slowly, very carefully, because she could not afford to make one mistake, she began to cut.

DEMETER

"I ask you for your compassion as I begin to tell you my story," Mana said. "I pray that you won't be too harsh on me. I pray that you remember I am simply a mother. And I pray for your forgiveness."

Mana looked out into the three waiting faces. She took a deep breath and began.

"My name was Demeter. Yes, Demeter. Goddess of the grain, I believe I was, corn, if you want to be specific, but basically I was responsible for everything that grew on the earth.

"I was the first one to speak the language of growing things. I was the one who instructed a rose how to smell. Smell like warm rain, I told it. Smell like a little girl. And it opened in my hand, alive and shivering, as it grew and partook of the sunlight.

"I was full, you see—in here." Mana tapped her chest. "In here, lived all the colors of the world. This was my gift. Perhaps that's why they called me a goddess. But really, I was simply a woman. A woman who was born with the colors of the earth inside her. I took those colors out of myself and painted the trees green, the poppies red and the sky a brilliant, piercing blue. And all the time the earth was whispering in my ear, 'There, that flower, how about pink?' There was always something that needed my touch.

"'All right,' I would say, and I would paint that flower with all that was inside me, until it bent over, so heavy with pink that it ached and cried out with the echoing and swirling of all that had come before, as it remembered the seashells, roses and cantaloupes that lay buried in its memory. I teased it into life, into a glorious symphony of what it means to be called pink.

"After I finished each masterpiece, I would collapse on the ground, dizzy, breathless. You see, each time, it took everything out of me to give that color up. I was a true painter. The world's first, I guess you could say. I painted with the colors of my soul.

"Can you imagine, being born to do that?" Mana gave a great laugh.

"And when I was Demeter it was always like this." Mana gestured in front of her. "It always smelled this good. Every day was summer, and every night was warm and welcoming. The earth was filled, overflowing. Everything I touched bloomed.

"I thought I could not possibly be any happier than when I was a young woman, painting the earth. We loved each other as nobody else, the earth and I. I never thought anybody or anything could come between us, until I got pregnant.

"The earth knew before I did. 'It will be a girl,' the earth told me. It was then that things began to change.

"I began to dream about the things I would do with my little girl. I began to dream about how we would laugh together, about how I would take her up into the hills and proudly show her the red rocks and antelope-colored canyons I had painted. I also started to dream about food. Things like peach cobbler and asparagus with butter all of sudden became very important to me. I had fantasies about cannisters of flour, barrels of rice and cornmeal. And cupboards to put the food in and a roof to keep that food dry. Windows, a fireplace and doors.

"You must understand that this was all very new. Food and shelter had never been important to me. But now that a baby was coming, everything had changed. I began to make lists of everything I needed.

"It was clear to me that I couldn't continue to sleep outside, anymore. Even though the nights were warm where I lived, I couldn't take the chance that the baby might catch cold, get sick. So I started dreaming about a stone cottage with wild rose bushes and columbine growing beside the front steps. A cottage with a green wooden door. And in that tiny cottage there would be two small rooms. A room for her with a bed piled high with pillows and a glorious quilt. And another room, a kitchen where we would eat dinner together in dishes the color of egg yolks.

"We would be so happy. We would need nothing but each other. Ah, yes, I began to dream about the daughter I would have. And then nothing was ever the same.

"She came finally. And it was you, Temu. Your name back then was Persephone. I have a feeling you remember," said Mana, looking at the red haired girl. Temu nodded, her eyes filled with tears.

"The moment you were put in my arms, I knew the reason I had been born. It was not to paint the earth, after all. I was born to be a mother.

"Persephone was my ultimate masterpiece. She was born out of the colors that grew inside me. There was no doubt—this daughter had risen whole from my soul. But then I was handed another bundle wrapped in white cloth.

" 'What's this?' I asked. 'It's your second daughter,' they told me.

"'Another?' I gasped. 'You must be mistaken. I've only given birth to one daughter. There must be some mistake.'

"'There's no mistake,' I was told. 'You've had twins,' they said, then left me alone to meet my second daughter.

"'Twins? In a matter of seconds my entire fantasy had changed. Two daughters? Well, this would be even better! We would really be a family with three of us. The two girls would fit just perfectly in that bed. I pulled back the blanket from my second daughter's face. And let forth a scream. For what lay under that blanket was an animal.

"I am not exaggerating. Really, she was truly hideous, and believe me you would have screamed, too. She had the face of a monster—a squished up nose, more like a snout, really, and she had whiskers on her chin. She looked nothing like her sister. She did not even look human. She had arms and legs, yes, but her body was short and muscular, and she was covered in black hair.

"And there was her smell. She didn't smell like a baby smells. No, this child smelled like something bad, something ruined. Her breath was not sweet like Persephone's, her breath stank of blood and game. She smelled like something wild. She was making little grunts and when she smiled at me her gums were black and spotted and she had teeth as sharp as fangs.

"'This is not my child!' I screamed. 'There's been some mistake! Take this thing back.' And I covered the beast's head with the blanket. Those little furry hands reached out to me, but I turned my head away.

"Nobody came running when I screamed. I was alone. The midwives had left—their work was done, for the birth had taken place.

"I looked around frantically. They had left food out on the table for me, there were candles lit and a pile of clean sheets next to me on the bed. It was warm and inviting in that birthing house, a woman's place, a safe place, but all I could think of was that I had to leave. I had to get myself and my daughter—the daughter I had dreamed about—to that stone cottage with the green wooden door, where the roses and columbine already grew high up the front steps.

"Slowly and carefully I got up, holding Persephone tight to my chest. I was bleeding, I had been split wide open in giving birth and I could feel the blood running down my legs as I stood. I could smell iron in the air. I could smell it strongly on my hands, and I remember thinking, oh, yes, that's the smell of blood.

"In the midst of those thoughts, I did the unspeakable—I took that baby animal and brought her with me outside. There was a forest behind the birthing house. I didn't have to walk more then fifty feet before the trees were dense, before I was in a green, mossy place where the sun didn't shine.

"The animal was quiet. She did not cry. She did not utter a word as I bent down and laid her under a tangle of raspberry bushes, clutching my precious Persephone in my arms.

"I had a sense that she knew exactly what I was doing—that even though she had just slipped out of my womb, she knew she was about to be abandoned.

"Her silence still persecutes me. I wanted her to howl, to scream, to do something at the injustice of her mother leaving her to die, but she said nothing. She let me go, her eyes wide open under the blanket.

"I remember cooing 'my real daughter' to Persephone as I began the walk home. I don't know how I made it. I was almost in shock, but I remember holding that sweet baby to my breasts. I remember thinking what a miracle it was that her mouth knew how to find my nipple. I grimaced as I thought of that dark, hairy child doing the same. And it was then that I began to deny the reality of those births. 'I only have one daughter,' I chanted. 'One daughter.'

"You see, there was no place in me that could understand how I could have given birth to that animal, to that beast, to that monster. It was a sick joke. That child looked nothing like me—anyone could see I couldn't possibly be her mother.

"But deep inside me, I knew the truth. That animal had, indeed, slid out from between my legs, right on her twin sister's heels. I also knew that the two of them had spent nine months together in the womb. But it had been dark in there, perhaps they couldn't see each other. Perhaps they couldn't see how different they were. Or maybe it didn't make any difference in the womb. They were twins, after all. Perhaps they loved each other fiercely for the simple reason that each was what the other was not.

"I told myself it didn't matter. All memory they had had of one another would have been erased the moment I pushed them out into the light.

"You see, I just couldn't stand to see myself as I really was. I saw Persephone as a reflection of myself, an extension of myself, made from all the best things that I was. But the animal, she just didn't fit. I was not dark and hairy, I did not grunt and moan or have saliva hanging in long threads from my chin. I was indignant about it. I never had been and never would be like that animal, so how could I possibly be her mother?

"Persephone and I went to live in our cottage. Those were the best days of my life, watching her grow. I told you, I was born to be a mother, and once Persephone arrived, I stopped painting. Raising a child, being a mother, was a full-time job for me. I didn't want to miss out on a moment of her growing up.

"She was the most delightful child. Truly a child of the sun. The two of us were inseparable. We did everything together. We were best friends, as well as mother and daughter.

"I made her the most magnificent dresses, I cooked her the best, most wholesome foods. Each morning we would wake early, when it was still dark, and climb far into the hills to watch the sun come up. Our days were filled with exercise and good food, with me teaching her the names of the plants and flowers. Her love for the earth came naturally. That was something I never had to teach. She was born with it. The ability to speak the language. Often I would catch her in conversation with some animal, a field mouse, or a shrew. And I would lie down on the grass and join her, the two of us giggling, our hair spread out on the lawn.

"And what of the beast, you wonder? What happened to her? To be honest, I wasn't sure what had happened to the animal. At first I assumed she would just die, being left there alone. I figured that was probably for the best, but mostly I just didn't allow myself to think about it. But there were many times during those years that Persephone and I were together, when I would often get the feeling we were being watched.

"It would happen at the most tender times between the two of us, the times that really speak of what it means to be mother and daughter—the times when I would be combing Persephone's hair after she had gotten out of the bathtub, the windows all steamy with heat—the times after dinner when she would curl up in my lap and I would read to her, breathing in the fruity smell of her skin, my chin resting on the top of her head—the times when we stood in the kitchen, on a Saturday morning, each of us kneading loaves of bread. 'More flour,' I would instruct her and then feel those eyes on my face. I would spin around to catch whoever it was, but there was never anybody there.

"I think some part of me knew who it was, knew who I would find standing there if I walked outside and looked behind the trees. I knew how that animal smelled. She had a musky, deep smell that was fringed with hay and shit. I knew those liquid brown eyes as well as I knew my own, the eyes that looked into those steamed-up windows with anger and rage and utter sadness.

"But I turned that knowing right off, pouring all of my love onto Persephone. I put everything I was into Persephone so that when she was taken, my world just fell apart.

"I know now that paying all this attention to Persephone was not healthy. I was the mother of twins, and I had love enough, as I had milk enough, for two, but because I only had Persephone, she got all the mothering that was inside me. I fear it was a little too much, because, to put it mildly, I had a hard time letting go.

"Ah, but you know how that part of the story goes. . . You know about that meadow. You know how she was dragged under. You know about the six black horses and the earth closing up as tight as a seam. My earth, my beloved earth, even she betrayed me, or so I thought, being party to my only daughter's abduction.

"I wandered the earth for nine days and nights. I barely knew who I was. I began changing. I tore my hair out in great chunks, my skin slackened and hung loose on my bones. I was covered in grime and stunk of my own feces.

"I became unrecognizable. Far from looking human, moving closer, closer to what I had denied I was. I moved down. I moved further in. I was not buried under a mile of dirt, but felt as if I was.

"Nothing was the same anymore. Nothing seemed to matter without Persephone. She was all I had, and without her, my life seemed meaningless. Without her the wind turned cold and bitter and the leaves were whipped off the trees, the flowers began to die, and my earth began to turn brown.

"'Why have you done this!' I screamed at the earth. 'Why have you betrayed me!' But the earth didn't answer. She was closed up tightly. She had shut her doors to me. She just turned darker and darker, and as she did, so did I.

"I began to experience feelings I had never known existed. I began to feel rage. Like a thick poison, seeping through my skin, rage came in. It entered me with a cackle, and it filled up my body. I began to scream, lifting my hands to the sky.

"Birds fell in their flight—soft, plump bodies hitting the ground without a sound. Soon it was raining tiny gray birds. The sky was filled with them, and I still had my arms raised up high. I wasn't sure if the birds were dead. Their eyes were closed when they hit the dirt, but they seemed to be more in shock, stunned, rather than dead.

"Ha! I thought, serves you right! How dare you cross me! Beware. *See what I can do!* I threw the rage up into my arms and sent it reeling into the air. Everything I pointed at began to die, began to wither, began to bleed the color I had so lovingly given it.

"I was crying, I was laughing. I was crazy, hysterical. I couldn't seem to stop myself. I had to use that rage up. And there was so*much* of it in my body, I thought it would never end. I had had the power to create this beauty, now, I also had the power to destroy it. And destroy it I did. When it was over I was spent. I fell on the ground, not sure if I would ever move again.

"When I looked up, when I raised my head from my arms, I saw that my world was one shade of gray. I had sucked the earth dry of the colors I had given her—the colors from my soul. The sky was a soundless scream. The ground was littered with birds.

"But as I lay there on the ground, smelling the scent of my unwashed body, I felt a strange sense of relief, as if a storm had just passed through me. I was exhausted, but my breath was solid and even, coming from deep in my chest. I felt clean, clear, yet I was the dirtiest I had ever been in my life.

"It was peaceful there, face down on the cold earth. I turned onto my back and looked up at the sky. It was a white sky without a touch of blue. At first my heart ached with missing the blueness, but as I continued to lie there, I realized that the whiteness provided its own strange comfort. Then the earth spoke.

"'Finally, you have come,' she said. I said nothing. I couldn't speak.

"'Don't worry about Persephone. I have her here with me. It's not so bad down here, you know. But you don't know, do you? You've never been down. You've never seen this part of me.'

"'I tried to tell you, Demeter.' The earth gave a heavy sigh and the ground shook beneath me in vibration. 'But you wouldn't listen. I would have preferred you came to this darkness, to this part of yourself of your own accord, but you were unwilling. You wanted to stay in the light. You were innocent, you were untouched and you wanted so desperately to stay in the light.'

"'Can you blame me?' I cried, finding my voice. 'I knew the light. And I knew it to be safe and to be good. In the light, everything grew. In the light, my daughter and I lived together, never separated. In the light we were mother and daughter forever, and the world went on around us, unchanged!'

"'But didn't you feel you were missing something? Didn't something feel. . . incomplete?' The earth asked gently.

"I shook my head. I didn't want to hear her words. 'The wind was always warm, and when it rained, it only rained for ten minutes at a time. Everything was perfect, whole. We were complete.' I insisted.

"'But did you really think you could spend your entire lives like that? What would happen when Persephone grew up? When she became a woman herself? She is already a woman, Demeter, haven't you noticed?'

"'She's not!' I snapped. 'She's nothing but a child.'

"'Oh, Demeter,' the earth sighed, 'My daughter. I have given you so much. I gave you the gift of color, and I taught you my language. But my greatest gift to you, the gift I really outdid myself with was the twins. I was quite pleased with myself over that one, you know,' the earth chuckled. 'I thought it was a perfect way to show you what you needed to be shown, to help you make your passage to the next stage of your life as a woman. And so I gave you a perfect set of twins. One dark. One light. Each one born of my body. And together, they made a whole. Together, they would have made *you* whole. But you refused my gift of wholeness, and you left the dark twin to die.'

"I was sobbing as she told me this story. She was absolutely right. She said what I knew to be true. I had refused to take her gift of wholeness. I was not ready to see both sides of myself. Some part of me had known I was looking at myself when I first set eyes on that baby's face. Some part of me knew that she and I had the same breath and that we both smelled of shit. But I much preferred to see myself only in the sweet apricot lips of Persephone. In the fruity smell of her skin.

"'Don't cry so, Demeter. The dark twin didn't die.'

"'But how could she have lived? She was just a baby!'

"'I took care of her, of course,' said the earth. 'Did you think I would let her die? I took her in my arms, and I held her, and I fed her mashed blueberries and peaches and gave her milk from the young goats.'

"'And, and she's alive now?' I stammered.

"'Alive and grown. Weighs nearly three hundred pounds,' said the earth. 'And she's watching us now from behind those trees.'

"I spun around and stared into the trees, and sure enough I felt the hair on the back of my neck rising, as it had done so many times when Persephone was growing up. So many times that poor beast had watched us from the trees.

"'She must hate me,' I said. 'She must want to kill me.'

"The earth shrugged. 'I don't know.'

"My head sunk down to my chest. 'I will let her kill me. I deserve it. It's the only way I can forgive myself. For what I have done to her . . . and to me.'

"I got up and walked towards the trees. I stopped when I was ten feet away, sank to my knees and threw my head back, exposing my neck to the white sky. Within seconds she was there, holding my head brutally in her big hands, her lips peeled back, her fangs exposed, ready to rip my throat open with one smooth sweep of her jaws.

"Do you think I was brave? To offer myself to the beast like that? I was not brave. I was a coward. I shit in my pants as I sat there, feeling her breath so close to mine. Everything let loose in me, my bowels, my bladder. I waited for what I thought would be the sound of my flesh being ripped open. I waited for the hot spurt of blood that I would feel as it fell upon my breasts.

"But it never happened. Instead, she threw back her head and uttered the most mournful cry. It was a cry steeped in pain, steeped in the hot, heavy pain of hundreds of years. I opened my eyes as she held my head in her hands. Her breath smelled like a room in which a woman has just given birth.

"I cried with her for her pain ran through me as if it were my own. The beast shook and she shuddered, she wailed and moaned, holding me, her mother, in her arms, and finally, that three hundred pound daughter of mine sank to the ground in exhaustion.

"Now, *I* am a big woman. Not three hundred pounds, but still a big woman. I was sobbing as I rolled her over, lifted her arms. I staggered to a standing position with her on my back.

"Her arms were long and hairy and they were wrapped around my neck, hanging down almost past my waist. I pulled her legs around me so she was sitting piggyback like a child. She gave a little cry at the tenderness of this position and then laid her head against my back.

"I began to walk. I had the strength of ten thousand women. I carried my dark daughter as if she were a feather. I carried my dark daughter, I carried myself. I carried us both way up into the hills and stopped only when I had found what I was looking for.

"It was a flower. The first flower I had ever painted pink. It was crumpled and withered, long past life. I wasn't sure if I could do my magic anymore. I felt completely drained. Still, I would try. I motioned for her to watch. I closed my eyes and slowly, slowly, summoned the pink of seashells and roses up through my soul. The flower once more blossomed magnificently, shaking with moisture, bending over again with the weight of the thick color and my daughter clapped her hands.

"'Do it again,' she roared.

"I took her face in my hands and pressed my cheek against hers. I had to laugh. She was so easily delighted.

"'I will do it again, 'I told her. 'And again, and again. I will paint the entire earth with you at my side.' I bent down and picked her up. For she was frail and weak, my beast, this child of mine, so filled with sadness.

"I carried her on my back."

❖ ❖ ❖

House sat in the rocking chair, under a bright light and hummed. If she listened hard, she could hear them outside on the raft, but she hummed over their voices. She didn't want to hear what they were saying. She had a dress to make.

All the pieces had been cut. Now it was time to pin. She got down on her hands and knees and spread the pieces out. She rubbed the polished wood of the floor with her fingertips as she ran the finished picture of the dress through her head, thinking about which part she should start first.

House loved to sew. She moved into another space when she sewed. House loved to take her time, anticipating the texture of the cloth. Then she would feel the cloth, feel the weight of it against her fingers. And she would listen hard.

The cloth would tell her then, it would whisper to her what it wanted to be. House would begin to fashion it, she and the cloth working together. She considered herself an instrument, with the finished work as the masterpiece. The fabric had known from the beginning what it wanted to be. Her job was simply to make sure it became that.

House got down on her hands and knees and she began to pin.

5

PERSEPHONE

"I remember my sister," Temu said. "I remember her when we were in the womb. We didn't talk, then. We just wrapped our arms and legs around one another, and pulsed there, forehead against forehead, swaying back and forth in the dark. I always thought that was just a dream, this holding of one another in the womb. I never knew where we were. And I never knew who she was. You were right, Mother. It was dark in there. But I would have loved her anywhere. Even in the light."

Temu dropped the blanket from her shoulders and stood up in front of the other women. Her eyes were glazed, her hair in ringlets. She stared out into the water.

"So, this is starting to make sense to me now—why I was pulled down into the earth. It was time for me to move down into the darkness, into *my* darkness.

"My abduction forced you to go down, too, Mother. It was a loss of innocence for both of us, wasn't it, not just me? We are no longer just creatures of the light, we are creatures of the dark as well. And having claimed that part of ourselves, we make ourselves whole.

"Mother, you mustn't think I hate you for what you did. I understand, because I, too, went kicking and screaming into the dark. I didn't walk willingly. I fought it every inch of the way. I fought the darkness rising in my mouth. I fought the dirt spilling into all my openings, my ears, my nostrils, between my legs. I screamed when I saw the rats, when I saw the worms and spiders. But most of all, what I fought, was the fading of the light. Until I heard what was at the bottom of it.

Temu flushed then, and even in the darkness they could see the red and pink splotches coming out all over her freckled body. "He had a voice like no other's. He spoke in symphonies, he spoke the language of the darkness.

"It was a language I had known once—for I was born out of it—

it was the language of the womb. Watery, self sustaining and protective, and at the same time utterly compelling. I couldn't help myself, Mother, I had to go to him. There was nothing in this world that could have kept me from that voice.

"He pulled me down to him with his hands." Temu flushed again. "I got hot and sweaty when I felt his hands on my body. A tingling in my breasts, a flood of water between my legs, and an emptiness in my heart. This is what struck me the most. I felt an emptiness in my heart.

"It was as if somebody had just shot a hole straight through me and now the wind was blowing through that hole. Strange, isn't it, I never imagined love would feel that way.

"But, you see, what happened was that when he placed his hand on my ankle my heart swelled, literally swelled, to three times its size. So big, my heart grew, in anticipation of the love it felt sure was coming. The feeling of emptiness was the the waiting-to-be-occupied space my heart, forever after, would continue to make."

Temu was crying as she spoke.

"He was the most beautiful man I had ever seen—emerald eyes and skin the color of a penny. He was tall, slim, but muscular. He told me he had been waiting for me his entire life.

"I believed him, Mother, because I looked in his eyes. I knew in that moment as he stared back at me, as the wind went whistling through the empty space around my heart, that we were meant to be with one another."

"What was it like down there?" asked Arian, softly.

Temu sighed and closed her eyes, remembering.

"There, the sun had always just set. Dusk was the lightest it ever got. It was dusk in the morning when I woke and dusk when I went to bed. I remember just images—faded ribbons, pale blue and yellow. Things that hang: strings, ropes, the red lacing off a well-loved softball. Long roads, roads that had no end, lined with columns of tall, elegant trees whose trunks gleamed purple in the night. And always there were the echos of voices, faint remnants of ancient conversations, moving about my ears.

"The rivers were the color of a bruise, dark blue and indigo, glowing, hissing around my ankles and gathering me in. Cool, cool water that helped me to remember, to move deep into what I knew to be true. The banks that lined those rivers were soft, yielding. Bats as small as swallows moved through the rushes; bird's nests dotted the shore; lacy moss hung down from the branches of the trees. The sun became nothing but a memory.

"I sat in open windows. I wore ice-blue gowns, wide skirts that rustled, sang to me. I walked on balconies. Lost all sense of time. I remember a bottle of wine being uncorked, the smell of cedar and vanilla in my nose as it was poured into a crystal glass. Rich merlots, dark burgundies running in streams down my breasts, my ribs being strummed like a guitar. And him, it was always him, walking beside me, whispering in my ear."

Temu's eyes snapped open. Her face was sharp, it had lost the soft edges of youth.

"I have grown, Mother, I have grown," said Temu, turning to stare at Mana. "Can you see," she said urgently. "It is dark here, like it is there. *Can you see* ?"

Mana was crying silently. She looked up and nodded.

Temu nodded back at her, then looked up into the night.

House picked up the pieces from the floor and tucked her sewing basket under her arm. She went outside to the porch. The rocking chair was there, all ready for her, an afghan folded neatly over the arm. She settled in with a sigh. This was her favorite part. She would work by the light of the stars.

She took out her needle and thread.

And began to sew.

6

ARIAN

"The women who have come before me have laid themselves down in my bones. My great-grandmother, my grandmother and my mother; they have laid themselves down in my bones. In the unnamed places within my breastbone, my sternum and my ribcage, lives their pain. Their pain—I will always carry, for I know, now, that it was from this pain that I was born. The pain of my ancestors, the fear of the darkness of their skin, of their religion, of whatever it was that made them *not the same*. Their oppression and cultural annihilation are buried in my bones. And I can not abandon my bones."

7

GREAT GRANDMOTHER

They took the men first.

"You must not be so beautiful," were the last words my husband said to me before running the razor-sharp edges of a stone against my cheek. Blood came immediately, and I gasped. He laced his fingers through mine, the blood thickening as it came out of the wound, darkening both our hands.

The scar did not serve to mar my face, to make me ugly, make me safe, as he thought it would. If anything, it added to my beauty, a fragileness around the eyes, a tenderness at the corner of the lips. Perhaps if I had been cut by my persecutors, it would have been different, a slicing of my face by one of them would have surely gotten infected, filled with pus, hardened to a thick, worm-like rising of the flesh. But it was my husband who ran the sharp edges of a stone over my face, thinking he would save me from things too horrible to speak of, and no scar born of love like that could turn me ugly. I wished it could, because if I were ugly, I might be killed quickly.

But I was beautiful, and so, an example would be made of me. I would be raped and sodomized, tortured, before I was killed; my nipples cut off, a knife jammed up between my legs. If I was lucky, I would be found by just one soldier, who would keep me for his own pleasure, sparing me from a multitude of rapes. But if God was not watching over me that day, then I might be raped by eight, ten of them, before I would be killed.

Yes, I knew exactly what my fate would be, because this had happened before. Twenty years ago, it had been the same thing.

I was ten years old on the day they dragged all the women and children from their houses into the middle of the village square. I was separated from my mothers and sisters immediately, for I was just a child. My mothers and sisters were in a group by themselves. They were beautiful women; lustrous hair, lips—the color of dahlias, almond eyes, golden skin. There was no denying their beauty.

I remember the smell of lamb and mint, the breath of the man who pinned back my arms as I was forced to watch my mother and sisters raped and then killed. Five men taking turns with them. All of us who were left, women, children and old men, screaming, screaming, mouths open, but no noise coming out.

I remember only in fragments. Falling, they fell in slow motion, like sunflowers, their bodies heavy in death, ankles turning, piles of blue-flowered cotton in the dirt. One of my sister's breasts was bared, the nipple abnormally dark in the bright sunlight. My mother's dress was twisted up around her waist, her white cotton underwear in a ball around her ankles.

I remember seeing my sister's shoe. It had fallen off her foot and lay on the ground beside her. My sister had coveted that shoe. She had saved for six months to buy that fashionable pair, and now the shoe lay beside her dead body looking like something stupid. How silly we all were, thinking about such ordinary things, as if life was ordinary, as if we could depend on life's dull, slow march. How starkly ridiculous the yearning for those shoes seemed, when I saw my sister dead on the street.

I will never forget the sounds of their voices. They called to me, you know—my mother and sisters called my name over and over again, they clung to my name as if it had the power to save them, as the man with the breath of lamb and mint leaned down and whispered in my ear, "One day, you'll be that beautiful."

After they were dead, he pushed me out into the middle of the square. "Clean it up," he told me. I knelt down by my mother's head. My skirt darkened and blued with the matter of her brains.

So you must know, that when the men were taken for the second time in my life, I knew what lay ahead. We had only a few days. There was a soldier who already had his eye on me. He was darker then me, a long, full mustache and eyes that were green.

"You're mine," he hissed at me, when I was getting water from the fountain. I clutched the baby to my breast and held my daughter tightly by the hand. I walked away, knowing in a few days there would be no more walking away. I didn't know what else to do. I took my children to the river.

My daughter remembers what happened that day differently than I do. It's strange, isn't it, how two people can have such different recollections, and always about the most important things. I cannot tell you why it happens that way, why memory between mother and daughter can become so skewed, but I tell you, on that summer day, when the sun was a ball of red sitting on the horizon, three days before they tore us from our houses, before our city was set on fire and the desert floor was covered with our slain bodies— it was me who gave my baby to the river, not my daughter.

Under the stairs, beneath the floorboards, in barrels of flour, high up in the limbs of trees, a moon-less night; these were the hiding places that babies gave away. I would rather kill my baby myself then have her be killed at the hand of our persecutors. So I brought my children down to the river.

They let me go. They thought the river was a safe place, a women's place. The night before, I had lined the bottom of a basket with stones. On top of that, I had placed our laundry, dresses and skirts that I knew we would not be needing again. The next morning

I woke early and put some sweet wine into my baby's juice. When she was asleep, I laid her down in the soft cushion of clothes, kissing each tiny inch of her over and over again before I covered her lightly with my older daughter's best dresses.

You may wonder how I could have done this. You would know if you had the knowledge of what was about to come running through your veins as I did—the sureness of death, of rape and torture. There was not a choice. I did what I knew was best.

My daughter remembered some things right. I did take off my shirt. It took me a long time to be able to give my baby to the river. But it was she who sat up on the bank, her hand up over her mouth, as I waded into the water with the basket in my arms.

It's funny how time switches things on you. She remembers it was her. She believes I tricked her into doing the deed. She was there, yes, she watched—and that was enough to haunt me forever, to make a child watch such a thing—but I never, never, would have had her do it for me.

As I walked into the river, I was praying my daughter hadn't heard the baby stirring, because the wine had worn off and the baby had woken, just minutes before I took the basket into the river.

My daughter must have heard her. She must have seen the clothes moving as the baby's tiny hands and legs pushed up, as she tried to uncover herself, to reach for the sun. My daughter must have heard and seen something, and held herself, then, responsible for her sister's death.

I didn't expect this. That her witnessing the act would be almost the same for her as having killed her sister herself, but over the years, she convinced herself she had done just that. She came to believe that she had been the one to bring her baby sister into the river.

I have been locked away ever since. In a room where there is no light.

8

GRANDMOTHER

I remember, I remember, I remember—in threes. *Do not trip, do not trip, do not trip*, my mother told me. *Walk lightly, walk lightly, walk lightly*, so they will not hear. Make your steps soft. Carry your shoes. Do not look behind you—only forward.

Come quick, a tap on my shoulder in the middle of the night, a hand over my mouth, my face pressed to her breasts. Once. Once again. Then I am up, moving. No lights, no candles. We move in the dark. We are of the dark. It will be the darkness that will save us.

I think we are going together. It is the day after we have gone to the river, and I am too young yet to remember what I have seen. My mother throws a sweater over her shoulders and leads me out into the night. He is asleep. I see him, in our backyard, stretched out under the fig tree, his gun on the ground. Even from here, I can see his dark, drooping mustache. He looks as if he has a rat draped over his lip. My mother pulls me into the woods.

"Do not trip, do not trip, do not trip." My mother's sentences come out of her mouth in threes.

"Walk softly, walk softly, walk softly." She smells like orchids, some perfume my father bought for her in the city. Her breath is feathery, sweet, she is so beautiful. The night is a shroud around us.

We walk for a long time. "I'm tired," I tell her, whining.

"No," she whispers, pulling me, "You must go on."

Finally, my legs collapse beneath me, and we stop. I sit, my back against a tree. She kneels in front of me, slips off my shoes and rubs my feet in her hands. "Good feet," she names them. She pulls honeyed sweets and pistachio nuts, wrapped in a napkin out of her sweater pocket. My eyes gleam in the darkness—these are my favorites. She feeds the sweets to me, one piece at a time, kissing my eyes, my cheeks, my hands, the top of my head, with each bite. We pop open the pistachio nuts and leave the shells in a pile on the ground.

After the food, we walk again. I have more energy. I am pleased, so pleased to have this time with my mother, alone in the woods. I think I will never forget this night.

"Don't trip," she tells me, pointing to a root. Obediently, I walk around it.

Finally, we see light. I hear my mother sigh, and I sigh, too, because the light feels safe, warm, glowing at us from within the woods. I am excited. My mother leans down, and I shiver as she looks into my face. Immediately, she takes off her sweater and wraps it around my shoulders. She is wearing her nightgown, and I see her breasts clearly, as if she is wearing nothing, the cotton so sheer and thin, her nipples jutting out, this cool night in June.

She pulls my head towards her and kisses my hair. I feel her kiss soak into me, hear her breathe heavily, and then she stands up and tells me to go ask for some water. She is thirsty, she says.

I'd do anything for my mother. I run eagerly toward the light, and there is a woman standing there, in the doorway of a stone building. "Come," she says, her voice is soft and kind.

"We are thirsty," I call out. "Do you have some water?"

"That is something I have," she tells me, as I walk toward her. The door shuts behind me, and I am in that orphanage for the next ten years.

Ten years is a long time to think, enough years for memory to become skewed, and by the time I leave that place, I remember only two things about my mother; her breasts, and the day she made me take my baby sister into the river.

9

ARIAN

The rest you will understand now.

That day in my grandmother's kitchen, the day my mother was raped, was the day my grandmother became five again. You see, my mother had breasts which were exactly like *her* mother's.

Those breasts, the color lavender, these were my grandmother's triggers. When she found herself in front of those breasts, in front of a certain shade of lavender, my grandmother relived, over and over again, the moments when she saw her little sister's hand, reaching out to her from beneath the lace of her best dress.

The day her memory had turned and she started to believe her mother had made *her* carry her sister into the river was the day she had thrown her mother into a dark room in her heart, and swallowed the key whole. My grandmother thought she had locked her mother away for good. Until the day she saw her daughter's breasts, and the door began to creak open.

My grandmother knew there was only one way to keep it shut; by turning her back on those breasts which were so like her mother's. My grandmother abandoned her daughter that day in the kitchen, just as she thought her mother had abandoned her baby sister and herself. And the legacy was passed on.

It is here, now, that you find me. I have gone back. I went back as far as I had to go. Until I unearthed. Until I uncovered. Until I knew, with my own heart, what had come before.

My great-grandmother flings up her hands and covers her face when I push the door open. It has been a hundred years that she has been sitting in this room in the dark. The sudden light blinds her and is painful. She whispers my grandmother's name.

"Is that you?" she asks in a voice so afraid to hope, it makes me want to cry.

"No, it is your great-granddaughter," I tell her.

She says nothing, but a tiny moan escapes her lips. The room is empty except for the hard wooden chair upon which my great-grandmother sits. She is naked. She is also surprisingly young. I expected an ancient, withered lady. This woman is far from that. Her hair is shiny, thick, the color of chestnuts. I know this is exactly the way she looked on that day she brought her daughters to the river.

"Well," she says after awhile, "You look very much like your grandmother. "

"I do?"

"Yes.You have the same mouth."

She speaks with a slight accent, her voice is melodious and lilting. "Where is your grandmother?" she asks.

"She is dead," I say softly. "She died a few months ago."

My great-grandmother turns her head sharply to the wall as if an invisible hand has just reached out and slapped her. Her eyes flood with tears. Her lips pull back from her mouth, her white, straight teeth rise and fall as she cries. Her hands move up to her breasts, frantically she tries to cover them, her grief is making her feel exposed. But her hands are too small, her breasts are too big. Finally she turns her head into her shoulder and sobs.

I walk up to her, then, I kneel in front of her and touch the back of her head, gently. She moves her head against my chest. I hold this beautiful woman in my arms and rock her. I look into those almond eyes. I look at my great-grandmother, and I look at myself.

"It's not your fault," I tell her. She begins to cry even harder then, her head shaking in my hands. "Are you listening to me?" I say louder. "I know why you killed your baby. I know that you felt she had no chance to live. I understand! It is not your fault!"

I feel the words rising in me. Rising to a scream. I am aware that the words are big. I also know that this moment is big. That I am standing here in a room with my great-grandmother. A room in which we are the same age.

I hear a huge creaking, then. We look up, and we hear words, we hear voices.

Mayrig, Madre, Haha, Oum. The voices go on and on, the languages turn and twist in the air. *Ammijaan, Mama, Anya, Mat.* With each word I taste a fabric, a texture, a piece of land. *Moeder, Mor, Anne, Maa.* Rivers, lakes, oceans pass through me, over me. *Na, Matka, Mutter, Em.* Countries, continents, planets ride my skin. *Ba, Mère, Muchin.* Time buries itself in my backbone.

I listen carefully, not hearing my own language, yet I know who the voices are calling. When the voices pause, I know it is my turn. "*Mom,*" I say, and the creaking begins to swell, now, to rise, as my word, as my language, my mother-line, joins all the others.

I know, now, what that creaking is. It is the creaking of a million doors opening, of light flooding into a million rooms. A million rooms where all the banished mothers have been sitting. A million rooms into which all the daughters now come.

Some of the mothers are old, some of them are young. Some have been in those rooms for hundreds, even thousands of years, others only one or two. But, all of these doors—all of them—begin to open, as each daughter reaches back in time. Back and back, each one goes as far back as she has to go.

And calls her mother out.

House's needle was flying over the fabric. She was barely breathing. She had entered a space where nothing existed but that cloth between her fingers and the stroke she was making.

In that space she was calm. In that space her fingers knew exactly what to do. In that space the cloth put itself together, guiding her hands just so.

House moved with total absorption. All she heard was the delicate, yellow hum that soared her fingers upward, to a place that was raining the sun.

She gathered this rain in her hands and sewed it into the bodice of the dress.

❖ ❖ ❖

Something in the water caught Arian's eye. It was a flash of red, turning and twisting with the solid weight of a fish.

"What is it, Arian?" asked Urd, leaning forward. "What do you see?"

Arian peered intently into the water.

"I'm not sure. Something red."

"A fish?" suggested Temu.

"I don't think so," said Arian distractedly.

"Perhaps you should investigate," said Urd, "Perhaps that glimmer of red was for you. Better go see what it's all about."

Arian raised her eyebrows at Urd. Urd nodded at her. She stood up and dove into the water.

It was dark in the river. It was, after all, night, but Arian was soon used to the darkness and she dove further down, deeper and deeper into River's waters, feeling the water cool rapidly as she descended.

She looked up and saw the raft floating above her, a solid, square object. She could see Mana's feet dangling over the side. Arian felt safe at the bottom of the river. Even though the water was cold, she felt good. She had no need to breathe.

Once in awhile she got scared and found herself gasping for air. But then she would bury her hands in the cool white sand and there she found her breath. Then she saw the flash of red again, twenty feet away from her. It was a stream. She followed it.

It remained in front of her for a long time, just far enough away for her to not be able to see what it was. She sensed that the bit of color was testing her. Would she keep following? Would she give up and go back to the surface? Or would she try to rush it, to find out what it was before it was ready to show her?

Arian kept her distance until the red movement slowed. It stopped and it turned, waiting for her to catch up. She closed her eyes as she swam forward. When she felt she had arrived, she opened her eyes and saw a little girl floating in front of her.

Arian stared, her hand flying up to her mouth. She reached out and touched the girl. She was firm, she was real. She was missing one of her front teeth. She had on a green dress, and her hair was in braids with long red ribbons hanging from the ends. They were what Arian had seen flashing in the water, twisting and turning in the black waves.

The girl smiled. She was carrying a naked baby in her arms, a baby draped in faded lavender ribbon.

Arian was shocked, her heart pounding. There could be no mistaking who this little girl was. It was her grandmother, exactly the way she had been on that day when her mother had taken her to the river.

The girl laughed when she saw the look in Arian's eyes. She giggled and bounced the baby up and down in her arms. She was a beautiful little girl, Arian's grandmother, and her dress floated up for a minute around her face, exposing her white panties and black leather shoes. She pulled it down, her face exploding with laughter again and then extended the baby to Arian.

Arian took the baby in her arms and was surprised at the heaviness of her body. She had expected her to be light, full of nothing, being down at the bottom of the river. The baby's mouth began searching for Arian's nipple and clamped on gently before Arian could stop her. She began to suck.

Arian looked up, surprised. She wasn't sure if she should let the baby do this. She didn't have any milk. She questioned the little girl with her eyes. Her grandmother answered her with a clap of her small hands and a somersault in the water, her long, black braids moving slowly over her shoulders, like an afterthought.

The baby's lips on her nipple sent a tugging into her womb that made Arian gasp. She stroked the down on the baby's head, saw the lavender ribbon that had been so carefully wound around her arms and chubby body. This was a baby who was obviously well cared for. This was a baby who was loved.

"What . . . what, are you doing here?" she finally stammered.

"Looking after my baby sister," the girl said. "I couldn't let her live down here alone."

"Oh," said Arian. "Well, are you okay down here? I mean are you fed, are you happy? Don't you get cold?"

"River takes care of us," said the little girl, twirling her hair around her fingers. " She has always taken care of us." She nodded, her almond eyes solemn. "Mama's down here, too."

"She is?" asked Arian, stunned. "Well, where is she?"

"Oh, she's gone to get us dinner. We eat well here. River gives us mussels and sweet fish, and we get to sleep in beds of river grass."

"You do? Well, aren't you lucky," said Arian. "Do you think I might get to meet your mother?"

"You already have," said the little girl, looking dumbfounded. "Why you're the one who brought her here. Don't you remember?"

"*I* brought her here? When?"

"Just a little awhile ago. At least I think Mama said it was you." The little girl swam in a circle around Arian, touching her arms, picking up her hair and finally peering at her feet.

"Yes. It was you. Mama said you glowed green, that you had the moon in your belly. She says that you have brought us all together. She says that you were the one who led her out of the room she had been locked up in—the room with no light. And now we're together, here with River. We've become a family again, and here at the bottom of the river we will be that way forever. Mama said it was important to give you something before you left."

"Oh," said Arian. It was all she could say. She tried to let what her grandmother had just said take root in her body. Arian looked down at her chest. The baby was still sucking. She hated to pull her away.

"Don't worry, she will swim with you like that," the little girl told her. Arian followed her to a place at the bottom of the river that was marked with a stick on which a pale blue dress was tied like a flag.

The little girl began to dig, then offered what she had uncovered to Arian. It was a pile of blue, shattered sky. It gleamed and glistened and turned into liquid in her small hands.

"I'm supposed to give it to you," said the little girl. "This belongs to your mother. Mama says it's high time it makes its way back."

"Your mother is a wise woman," said Arian, handing the baby back to her grandmother. Then she knelt on her hands and knees and scooped up those pieces of sky. They shivered in her hands and Arian began to float to the surface of the water.

"Bye, byyyeeeee," she heard her grandmother's voice from the bottom of the river. Arian went up, faster and faster, and broke the surface with such speed she flew ten feet into the air. She flung her hands open, tossing the blue pieces into the air like birds. Then she sank back into the warm water, watching as those pieces floated back up to where they had once been.

It was like fireworks. They all watched, their heads tilted until the last blue spark melted into the big night sky.

10

HECATE

"Well," said Urd, rising to her feet. "I guess it's my turn." The old woman remained wrapped in her blanket and she turned around and looked at each one of them for a long time. Then she sat down again.

"I'm too old to stand for that long," she told them. "Besides I like the idea of a circle now. That's what we've become—a full circle. " The old woman sighed heavily and pulled her blanket tight around her neck.

"I am Hecate, she who stands at the crossroads. The one who watches, the one who witnesses."

Temu, Mana and Arian had suspected who Urd was, but when she confirmed it, they all shivered and pulled their blankets more tightly around them.

"I am the one who brought you all together. I am the one who asked you to go down into your depths. I encouraged you to go individually, at first. The stories you just told were about your individual descents."

Urd's bright eyes glowed at them out of the darkness of her face.

"Now that you have heard those stories, I think it should be clear to you that you all have something in common. Temu, do you know what that is?"

Temu nodded. "It is our pain," she said.

"Yes. It is your pain. Pain that has been handed down from generation to generation. This pain is so widespread, so big, that it has become what will bind us together. From every continent, from every country, from every city, town and village, we will begin to gather, as we are gathering here, and we will start to hear the telling of the stories. We will*all* take on the burden of the pain, lessening the burden on each individual. The voices will finally be allowed to speak, and the healing will begin.

We have carried this pain on great backs and strong thighs for decades, for centuries, for thousands of years. The pain of mother and daughter, of sisters, of cousins, of entire generations, of a planet. It is from this pain that we will begin to rise, and in the end it will be the uncovering and sharing of this pain, of this darkness, that will make us whole."

Urd put her hand up to her ear and cocked her head.

"Listen!" she whispered. "Can you hear it?"

Mana, Arian and Temu listened closely. They did hear something. A new sound in the night, a breeze rushing in.

"What is that?" whispered Mana. "Do you know?"

"I know," the old woman nodded. "And so do you. Listen."

They listened as the noise grew louder and louder, and soon they knew the noise for what it was. It was the sound of fresh air. The sound of women standing up, getting out of their chairs. It was the sound of freedom. The sound of compassion and forgiveness.

The sound was pounding, it was rushing, it was pumping through their veins.

They heard the voice of the future. They rose to their feet.

And they found that voice to be their own.

House was done. She held the dress up in front of her, and it floated away, right out of her hands. So light was the cloth, woven with sky and sun, that it danced around her head and House laughed. She tossed her head back and roared.

She had outdone herself this time. This dress was the most beautiful thing she had ever made. She had sewn it right out of her heart.

It was dotted with the lace from her soul.

PART SEVEN

A DOOR OPENS. . .

1

ARIAN

Well, this part of the journey is almost over. There is only one thing left for me to do, and I'm sure you know what that is. It is time for me to give the moon back to the sky.

Night has fallen. I speak to you one last time as *the girl who swallowed the moon*. Very soon, I will no longer carry the moon in my body.

I wonder what you will call me then. You probably won't even recognize me—at least not as somebody special. That's fine. That's what is supposed to happen. I could be the woman sitting beside you on the train, or the one in line at the grocery store. You won't see me as any different from yourselves after tonight. And for that I am glad.

Part of me is excited for this all to be over. I am ready to return to my ordinary self, to give up the responsibility of being the one whom the moon picked to carry her secrets.

They really aren't secrets, anymore. You heard those doors opening just as I did. You heard the air rushing in. And you know, now, that it is from you that I gather my strength.

Let me set the stage for you. Look with my eyes. Look one last time, and see the night as I am seeing it now. I am sailing down the river in a canoe. I sail alone.

You know where I am going. I am going back to that hill in the middle of the woods, in the clearing, to which I came so many nights ago and first saw the ladder hanging in the sky.

I know the ladder will be there again when I arrive, but this time there is no fear. There is nothing but the liquid gold rising and filling my mouth.

"Wait," I tell the moon. "Be patient, we are almost there." The moon pulses excitedly in the back of my throat. She is eager to be back in the sky.

It is a beautiful night. See with my eyes. Yes, I am barefoot. But wait, what is that lavender and purple hem that you see dancing across my ankles. I show it to you up close and you gasp. I am wearing a dress made of lilacs. You smell the lilacs now and the sweetness of them fills the night. You feel the silky petals brushing against your bare legs as they are brushing against mine. Your hand rises and moves to your breast. There, the dress is woven with the sun. It is warm and full of heat, this material covering your body.

Your heart aches. You want the dress for your own. Here, take it. It is a dress that came from my dear House's soul, and I want you to know how it feels on your body.

They all gave me gifts before I made my way into the night. Each one gave me something very special that I take with me on this last part of my journey.

Persephone gave me a handful of pomegranate seeds. Wrapping them in a piece of cloth, she told me to carry them close to my heart. "Eat them," she told me," and you will remember who you were."

"How could I possibly forget?" I asked her.

"Oh, you'd be surprised," she answered. "But if you find yourself in danger of forgetting, all you have to do is swallow one of these seeds, and we will all come back."

Demeter gave me a narcissus. I was surprised at first, but as she pinned it in my hair she explained.

"This narcissus represents freedom," she told me, as she swept my hair up into a braid. "I am a mother. You are a daughter. And as a mother I grant you, my daughter, your freedom. I grant you your life. I give to you the ability to go your own way. To separate from me. And in peace, I wish you to go to your beloved."

Demeter was crying as she told me this. Her tears spilled on my hair and sprang into pale pink blooms.

The last gift I was given was from the old woman.

"You were born from the darkness," she said. "And into the darkness you will move again, and so I give to you this night." The old woman spread her hands out wide, and night fell from her fingertips, sticky and fragrant. She spread the night out over the earth.

"Take this night," she said, "and ride it into the future. Don't ever forget that it is yours, Arian. For you were born of it and you are inextricably entwined."

They walked me down to the canoe, waited for me to climb in and then pushed the canoe off. Urd said, "I never was much for good-byes," and off I went.

Here I am now, here you have found me, as I sail downriver to the ladder.

Can you smell this summer night? Can you hear the crickets, the frogs? Can you see River swimming beside me silently, her black hair like silk on the water?

I kneel down on the wood of the canoe and my dress balloons around me. The dress is like the wind. I am naked underneath. I feel strong. I feel whole. I feel ready to let the moon go.

The canoe moves through the water like time. This movement is ancient—a girl in a canoe in the middle of the night. The wind blows my hair back from my face and I feel my mother. She is with me, sitting on my cheekbones.

The canoe bumps along the riverbank. I climb out, holding up the bottom of my dress. There is a path in front of me. My breath doubles back on itself, as does my memory. I have been here before. It is exactly the same.

I remember what it's like to be the dark. I throw off the dress and wrap myself around myself, blanket myself in the sweet molasses batter. I borrow night's cloak and throw it over my shoulders. I look magnificent, striding through the woods, traces of pink and purple sky streaming out behind me.

Wearing night's cloak gives me the courage to keep walking. Because I'm not walking *in* the night. I *am* the night. And I am not afraid. I look down at my feet, see them walking quickly, surely, firmly. I look down at my feet and I love those feet. I look down at my hands, each of them wrapped with rich sticky darkness and ice blue stars. I look down at those hands and I love those hands. And I look down at the curve of my belly, at my small, earth-colored breasts, at the tips of my hair hanging over my shoulders and I love my belly, my breasts and my hair.

And it is the night. It is night that hands these things to me, gives them back to me like a gift. I see myself then, for the first time, in the dark, and I love myself without a doubt.

I carry myself, I carry the night on my back. I carry us both through the forest and into a clearing where the noises are loud all around me.

The crickets sing of moist, green places, their songs right on the edge, where sad melts into sweet. It is a song of remembering, I know. The crickets sing the taste of corn, yellow and bursting with buttery silk. They sing the smell of strawberries in warm rain. They sing the song of mist, of morning, of twilight. They sing to help me remember.

I kneel down in the clearing and listen and finally hear the crickets' song. I let it pull me. I fall backwards into it. It is comforting and it is safe.

And I remember.

The sky is dark purple, black around the edges. It shivers and dances. Loving myself ferociously, I take the sky in my two hands and pull it down to me like a sheet. I fold the sky in half. It is big, this sky, cool and cavernous, like a shell. I step into it, one foot at a time, like stepping into pajamas. I pull the sky on, bring it up around my waist and knot it like a sash.

I am dressed. It suits me. I wear only the sky, slung low around my hips and the night as a cape on my back. My legs are strong and firm, my shoulders wide. My lips curve down at the edges and are the color of raspberries. I am slim, muscled, and I run like an animal, low to the ground and leaping, one hand sweeping my hair into a tail as I fly. I smell like pine sap; I smell like rock. I wear the sky and the night with the ease and familiarity of a second skin and I am all of these things and more.

Standing now, I lift my head. I am intensely aware of every part of my body, every stretch, every tendon. I can feel my bones settling within my skin, feel the skin holding me tight. It feels wonderful, the pull of my neck. Slowly and deliberately, I move my eyes upward.

And see the ladder, hanging like a planet in the sky.

Everything was exactly as it was that first night when I swallowed the moon. But as I stood there, staring up into the sky, the ladder stretching up before me, I realized *something* was different. This time I was not alone. This time I was surrounded by voices.

I looked around me, hearing the voices get louder. From mere whispers, they slowly grew to shouts. There were hundreds, no thousands, of voices.

"Climb!" they told me. "Climb for me, because I have no arms. Climb for me because I was locked in a little room. Climb for me because I could never find the ladder. Climb for me because I didn't have the courage!"

I did as they asked, and I climbed for us all. The higher into the night I went, the brighter and more glistening the night became. Violet flew into my eyes. I dug my fingers into the ice cold centers of the planets.

"Climb!" the voices screamed. "Never stop climbing!"

The moon was singing. The moon was singing arias, and I climbed into the night. I was breathless, I was daring, I was not looking where I was going.

My head slammed into the bottom of a door.

It was a door the color of eggplant. A door as dark as communion wine. The moon rose into my mouth then. She gave a little moan.

"Okay, Okay," I murmured. "Back you go." I swung the door open.

As soon as the door opened, the moon was at my lips, pouring herself out into the night. She sighed as she passed from me, and I felt myself filling with an emptiness I knew would never again be filled. It was an emptiness so gaping that it took my breath away. As the moon grew and rose to her place in the sky, I realized what the emptiness was. It was loss, grief—it was mourning.

The girl who swallowed the moon was gone. Standing in her place, there was a woman.

I looked down at this woman. She was a stranger, but familiar at the same time. I touched her. I touched her lips and her breasts. She had a strong, wide back and sturdy thighs. Her hair was long. It reminded me of the girl who swallowed the moon's hair, except that it was not quite as shiny.

She started to climb back down, and I screamed at her not to go. "You can't go, you just can't leave her up there!" I pointed to the sky.

"She's not up there anymore," the woman told me gently. "The girl who swallowed the moon is gone."

"Gone? What do you mean gone? She's coming back, isn't she? She wouldn't just leave me here alone!" I cried.

"She didn't leave you alone," the woman told me, her eyes smiling. "She left me in her place."

"You!" I shouted. "And who are you?"

"I am the woman you've just become."

"But I'm twenty eight years old!" I protested. "I've been a woman for years!"

"Age means nothing. You could be seventy years old and still be a girl. It has nothing to do with age. It has to do with your voice.

"Don't you see," she said. "I 'm here on this ladder because you have finally found your voice. You couldn't have swallowed the moon if you hadn't started that process, and you wouldn't have been able to let the moon go if you hadn't come through it completely. Arian, you are no longer a girl. You have seen far too much."

"Oh," I said, pouting. "But you're not as pretty or as special as she was. You certainly don't glow the way she did," I told her, looking into her eyes.

The woman laughed. "No, I don't," she said. "At least not on the outside. The moon no longer falls from my breath, but, Arian, you can be sure I am lit on the inside. I carry with me now, in my bones, in each one of my cells, the colors and the sights I have seen. They are a part of me. The night and moon are a part of me, as are those voices of all the women you heard down below. I have never been so connected, so far reaching, so big. And now I will take that knowledge back with me into the rest of my life. Now, I am ready to commit, to myself and then to a partner. Don't you see, Arian, you had to come here." The woman raised her eyebrows at me.

"Your Aunt knew about it. She sent you here, didn't she? She sent you here to live your last days as a girl, hoping you would leave here with your voice. And you've done that," the woman nodded, "because here I am. Now we must go back into the world and begin our work."

"But I want to stay up here," I whined, hanging desperately onto the ladder. "Here, on this ladder, I can still touch the moon. On this ladder there is House, there is Mana, Temu and Urd. On this ladder I can remember who I was."

"Ah, yes," the woman said. " I won't dispute that. Back down on the ground it will not be nearly so exciting. The world is simply not as bright as it is on the ladder. But Arian, you are human. If you stay up here you will die. Trust me, I know. You can't harness this kind of power, this kind of knowing. It's not yours to take. It 's only yours for brief moments in time—moments like this when you move from one stage of your life to another.

It will get easier, I promise you. The memory of this will fade. The ache in your belly will stop. You'll become satisfied with seeing the sun shining down on the earth with your mortal eyes. You will still smell the lilacs, but with your human nose. And these things will become precious to you again. These things you will never take for granted. But you can't stay here on this ladder. You are not of this world. It is time to climb back down to your own."

The woman held her arms out to me then, and I stepped into them. It was a melting feeling, like coming home, as I moved myself into her body and her voice. I climbed down through the night, each step taking me closer to the earth that I knew and loved. I became sleepier and sleepier the farther I climbed out of the night. I could barely make my limbs move. When I finally made it to the ground, I knelt and kissed the earth. I ran my fingers through the grass and lay down under a pine tree. I was asleep in minutes. I didn't wake until the following morning.

The air was still. My dress was damp when I put it on. I remembered who I was.

PART EIGHT

. . . AND CLOSES

HOUSE

She couldn't see me any more when she returned the next morning. I guess I should have expected that. I knew, when she went off in that canoe, wearing the dress that I had made her, that she would never see me again, but I hadn't wanted to admit it. I wanted things to go on as they had. I was so happy, so full. I made the mistake of thinking she was there for me instead of the other way around.

I heard her whistling and ran out to the porch.

"Arian, Arian!" I called. " Come quick, I've been waiting for you."

But she didn't answer.

"Arian!" I sang. "I made pancakes for breakfast." I could see her now. She was running down the hill. She was still wearing the dress that I had made for her, but it looked different—not nearly as shiny, not nearly as beautiful. As she got closer, I realized what had happened. The dress had died. The life had gone right out of it. It was no longer lilac, sun and wind. Now, it was just a bunch of old fabric, filled with moth holes and brown with age. I gasped.

"What happened?" I yelled, "The dress. It's dead." Arian walked towards me but not *to* me. She didn't hear me, didn't see me. It was true, then. I had become invisible to her, as I had feared I would.

I began to cry, my heart filled with the pain of knowing I was alone once again.

Arian walked right by me and into the kitchen. I grabbed her arm, but she didn't feel it, of course. She was smiling, humming. She looked bigger somehow. She looked changed.

The moon was gone from her belly, from around her mouth. She looked normal again, an ordinary human being. I followed her as she walked from room to room.

I didn't know how I was going to stand it. Just last night I was filled, every part of me complete and breathing. And then, one by one, they had all left. Temu, Mana and Urd went last night after they saw Arian off in the canoe.

"Our work is done," Urd told me. "We must move on."

I was heartbroken to see them go, but I understood. I knew what

Arian was going to do that night, and I knew they had come to see her to that place. So it made sense to me that *they* would go, but I hadn't expected Arian to leave quite so soon. A little time between departures would have been nice. Then I could have gotten used to the idea of being alone again.

The phone rang. Arian smiled and ran to get it. She still had the flower Demeter had given her tied into her hair, but it was not a narcissus anymore.This morning it was a daisy.

I heard the voice on the other end of the line—it was her beloved's voice. I could tell by the way her face softened as that voice called her back into her world.

"Come home," her beloved told her.

"Yes," she answered.

And she began to pack her bags. It didn't take her long. She took off the dress that I had so lovingly made and left it hanging on a peg. I picked the dress up and held it to my face.

"Wait," I whispered. "Don't we even get to say good-bye?"

But I knew the answer was no. How would I ever stand the silence? It seemed I had spent most of life alone. Wouldn't anyone ever come and stay?

I wiped the tears from my eyes. Don't be such a baby, I told myself. You're not alone. You have River, and you have yourself. I looked around then, up at my walls, and I could see all the laughter, all the tears and emotions we had shared. It was all floating there, wrapped around my beams.

I sighed heavily and watched her as she shut her suitcase. It felt so harsh, but this was the price she had to pay for walking through that door. There was a toll exacted for the journey—you didn't get to go through for free. You had to leave some part of yourself behind. And that something is me, my world. A place where food is always flowing, a place where you're never hungry, where someone always takes care of you. I am a magic world, a world where rivers talk and flowers still smell like love.

But, sadly, I am temporary. I am not a final destination. That world out there, the world in which the phone rings, is where Arian belongs. And at this moment, as she stands here in the kitchen, her bags in hand, taking one last look around, the door to the two worlds is open.

This doesn't happen very often. Hardly ever, really, and in some ways it's fun for me to watch. But it's also strange. I can feel her world blowing in through the windows and it makes me shiver. It is cold there. She has her work cut out for her.

Part of me wants to cry out and stop her. I could, you know. I could call to her in a voice she would remember. But it is not my place to do this. I comfort myself with knowing that she does not go back unprotected. She is going back with her voice. And so I do the final thing for Arian that I can do.

I step aside and let her go.

As the screen door slams behind her, sealing tight again the seams between the two worlds, the dress turns back into the sun and wind in my hands. It comes alive again in the echo of the still air. I carry it to the porch bedroom, tucking it into the drawer. I am content. It was a wedding dress, after all, in a world where girls still swallow moons.

And somewhere, in the distance, I hear an unmistakable sound —the sound of a door closing. A door the color of eggplant.

It is solid and unwavering, shut, in the middle of the sky.

Robert Bossi

Melanie Gideon is a graduate of Emerson College.
She lives in Massachusetts with her husband and is currently at work on her second novel.